Bolan jerked the wheel
and the Blazer slewed sideways

The vehicle dipped sharply as the front end slipped off the shoulder and chewed through a narrow gully.

"Rosie, you'll have to drive," Bolan yelled above the straining engine. "Get Anthony onto the floor and climb up here, quick."

As Roseanne braced herself on the back of the seat, Bolan put the pedal to the floor, and the Blazer spurted, widening the gap a little.

The warrior reached for the M-16. "Get ready," he growled. "Move over here." He pressed against the door, making room for Roseanne on the driver's seat. "Grab the wheel."

The Executioner knew he'd never get a better chance. He forced his door open against the wind and cradled the assault rifle. As the Blazer came out of the turn, Bolan hurled himself into the darkness.

D1024665

MACK BOLAN®

The Executioner

DON PENDLETON'S
THE EXECUTIONER®
FEATURING MACK BOLAN®

THE BIG KILL

A GOLD EAGLE BOOK FROM
WORLDWIDE®

TORONTO · NEW YORK · LONDON · PARIS
AMSTERDAM · STOCKHOLM · HAMBURG
ATHENS · MILAN · TOKYO · SYDNEY

First edition December 1989

ISBN 0-373-61132-3

Special thanks and acknowledgment to
Charlie McDade for his contribution to this work.

... There is too much grit in the money-machine. When money is the key to power some of the power will get into the wrong hands.

—John Wain,
Punch, Sept. 28, 1960

Ruthless people are always willing to spill that last drop of blood, all in the name of power. But this soldier will always stand at the end of the line and say "No. That's enough."

—Mack Bolan

THE
MACK BOLAN®
LEGEND

Nothing less than a war could have fashioned the destiny of the man called Mack Bolan. Bolan earned the Executioner title in the jungle hell of Vietnam.

But this soldier also wore another name—Sergeant Mercy. He was so tagged because of the compassion he showed to wounded comrades-in-arms and Vietnamese civilians.

Mack Bolan's second tour of duty ended prematurely when he was given emergency leave to return home and bury his family, victims of the Mob. Then he declared a one-man war against the Mafia.

He confronted the Families head-on from coast to coast, and soon a hope of victory began to appear. But Bolan had broken society's every rule. That same society started gunning for this elusive warrior—to no avail.

So Bolan was offered amnesty to work within the system against terrorism. This time, as an employee of Uncle Sam, Bolan became Colonel John Phoenix. With a command center at Stony Man Farm in Virginia, he and his new allies—Able Team and Phoenix Force—waged relentless war on a new adversary: the KGB.

But when his one true love, April Rose, died at the hands of the Soviet terror machine, Bolan severed all ties with Establishment authority.

Now, after a lengthy lone-wolf struggle and much soul-searching, the Executioner has agreed to enter an "arm's-length" alliance with his government once more, reserving the right to pursue personal missions in his Everlasting War.

1

The rumpled cop behind the wheel of the battered Chevy stared up at the glass-and-aluminum office tower that stabbed into the sky. The burnished metal letters that spelled out Fontanelli Industries glittered dully in the winter light. Three feet high, and centered over the two-story archway that led to the lobby, the letters seemed to scream for somebody to spatter a little mud on them, and that's just what Barry Novick had in mind.

Novick pushed through the revolving door, his feet rapping on jet-black marble laced with spidery webs of white and pink. He crossed the lobby at a half sprint, attracting the attention of two guards, who converged on him as he neared the elevator bank. One of the guards, a beefy, red-faced man who seemed to have had his mound of white hair modeled after the style of Tip O'Neill, blocked his path.

"You in a hurry, bub?" the guard asked.

"Bub? Did you actually call me 'bub'?" Novick asked.

"Don't be smart-mouthing me, wise guy. I eat guys like you for breakfast."

"Not me, bub. You try me, and you'll have indigestion for a year and a half." As he spoke, Novick reached into his jacket. He flashed his shield, and the guard cocked his head to one side.

"Why didn't you say so?"

"I didn't want to waste any time in the lobby," Novick snapped. "So, if you'll excuse me..." He stepped around the guard and into the elevator. As the doors began to close, he smiled at the guard and snapped off a crisp salute.

He punched the *P* button, which he knew must be the top floor, in the manner of swanky New York apartment buildings, where the *P* stood for penthouse. The car flowed upward so smoothly that it stopped almost before the homicide cop realized it was even getting close.

When the door slid open, Novick stepped onto a carpet so deep that it threatened to swallow his shoes. A huge teak desk, like the prow of a carrier, stood halfway down the hall. Three women behind it busily answered telephones and rapped on computer keys in some sort of dexterity test. It reminded him of the kid's game, where you tried to rub your head and stomach at the same time, in opposite directions.

With his hand on his ID case, he ambled toward the desk, a grin already settling into place. The woman in the center replaced her phone receiver and looked at him expectantly as he approached.

"Lieutenant Novick?"

"My fame preceded me, I see."

"How can I help you?"

"Who said you could?"

"I am the head receptionist." Her smile was blue-white, and if it got any colder, he'd have to wear mittens.

"Who receives the rest of the body?"

"I'm sorry?"

"I want to see Mr. Fontanelli."

"Which one?"

"Whichever one is in charge of prostitution."

"I don't think that's funny, Lieutenant."

"Neither will he."

"I'm afraid I have to know a little more about your business before I can direct you."

"Honey, the less you know about my business, the better you'll sleep at night. Just point me to either Fontanelli and forget I'm here."

She nodded curtly, then pressed a button on the massive phone console to her left.

Novick smiled at her flankers, neither of whom had struck a single key since he'd reached the desk. "You girls ought to try a little harder. There must be a letter or two for you to type."

A huge plate-glass window directly behind the massive desk provided a spectacular panorama of the mountains in the distance. Novick perched on the desk on one hip, drumming his fingers on the brightly polished wood. A moment later a tall man appeared in a doorway to the right. He looked around the reception area as if he weren't quite sure where he was.

Novick said to the head receptionist, "That must be a Fontanelli, am I right?"

"Yes, you are."

He slid off the desk and landed easily on his loafered feet. He rounded the desk and approached the tall man with a smile.

"Mr. Fontanelli? I'm Lieutenant Barry Novick, Homicide. I'd like to ask you a few questions, if I might."

"Of course, Lieutenant. Follow me, please." He turned crisply, with nearly military precision, and headed back the way he'd come. Novick fell in behind. The man was an impressive physical specimen, he had to admit. About six-one or -two, he appeared to weigh about one-seventy, but Novick knew how deceptive such things could be. He guessed Fontanelli was closer to one-ninety.

Fontanelli led the way into an office that was almost the antithesis of the reception area. The thick pile carpet was gone. In its place was polished wood and a couple of area rugs, the kind of Scandinavian modern abstracts that had been fashionable twenty years earlier. The furniture, too, was less than ostentatious. Functional, clean-lined and obviously inexpensive, it occupied no more than a fraction of the space of the office. The only evidence of opulence was the wall of books, and even they looked read rather than displayed.

Fontanelli noticed his gaze and said, "Please, don't ask me if I've read them all. I haven't, but I hope to."

He dropped into the desk chair and offered Novick a coffee which he declined. "I'll take a diet soda, though, if you've got one."

"Coke or Pepsi?"

"Whatever's on sale. That's how I buy it."

Fontanelli grinned easily. He pressed his intercom button, and soft static filled the room. "Janice, two diet sodas, two glasses and some ice, please." He listened for a moment. "Whatever's on sale," he said, hanging up.

Fontanelli leaned back in his chair, folded his hands behind his head and propped his expensively shod feet on the desk.

"Shoot," he said.

Novick reached into his pocket and pulled out a cardboard matchbook. A big-breasted and topless blonde pouted around a lollipop. Her full lips glistened, and the tip of her pink tongue curled around the candy. He nodded and tossed the matchbook onto the desk. The stiff cardboard skipped once and landed in Fontanelli's lap. "Look familiar?"

The executive fished it from his lap and examined it. "Good-looking woman. But no, I've never seen her."

"Not the girl, the matchbook."

"No, never seen one like it before. You collect them?"

"How about the company? Ladies in Waiting? That ring a bell?"

"Should it?"

"Yeah, it should."

"Tell me why."

Novick was about to answer when the door swung open after a tentative knock. He turned toward the door. "Ah, the head receptionist," he said.

Janice crossed the floor, her heels rapping on the hardwood. She carried a tray, balanced lightly on the tips of her fingers. The tray bore two cans of Diet Coke and a pair of glasses. The smile on her face was colder than the tinkling ice in the tumblers. She slipped the tray onto the desk without a sound.

"Thanks, Janice," Fontanelli said as she clacked back toward the door.

"*You're* welcome," she snapped. The door closed quietly on pneumatic hinges, despite her attempt to slam it.

Fontanelli pushed one soda toward Novick, then took a sip of the other. "You were saying?"

"If Ladies in Waiting isn't familiar, maybe you recognize Skylark?"

"No. Never heard of it. What, or who, is it?"

"Halcyon?"

"That I've heard of. It's one of our subsidiaries. Not a big part of the business, though."

"Laguna Hotels?"

"Now you're talking big money. That was one of our best acquisitions. What are you getting at?"

"I'm not sure."

"You said you were homicide?"

"I'll get to that in a minute."

Fontanelli nodded. "Okay, Lieutenant. However you want to proceed."

"I took a little trip yesterday, all on paper. And guess what I learned?" When Fontanelli said nothing, Novick continued. "Laguna Hotels is the owner of record of Halcyon Corporation. Skylark and Ladies in Waiting, however, have fronts. Both of them show the same thing. The papers on file only show they are operated by one Gino Marchibroda, as an agent for the owners. Unfortunately that's all the information necessary to file papers of incorporation. But if you pull on loose ends, they have a way of unraveling. Don't they?"

"I know Gino, if that's what you mean."

"I do, but I mean more than that. I also mean that Mr. Marchibroda is an attorney, as you well know. Not only that, he's on your corporation's board of directors, and he's your primary counsel."

"So?"

"So this—as an officer of the court, which he is as an attorney, Mr. Marchibroda was duty bound to reveal the name of the actual owners of both Skylark and Ladies in Waiting. Either that or risk disbarment by obstructing justice. He wouldn't want to do that. And I'm sure you wouldn't want him to."

"No, of course not. But will you please come to the point, Lieutenant?"

Novick reached into his coat again. This time he removed a brown envelope, from which he withdrew two photographs. He glanced at each, then slid the first across the desk to Fontanelli. "Ever seen her?"

Fontanelli picked up the picture and his face seemed to crumple for an instant then, in a miracle of recovered poise, it became as smooth as glass. "Yes, I do. Tracy Spillman. Or rather, I used to know her."

"When was the last time you saw her?"

"Not for several years. I'm not sure exactly, but I'd guess about six years ago, more or less."

"That's an old picture."

"Yes, it is."

"Here's a more recent one." Novick placed the second photo on the edge of the desk, then flicked it with a fingernail to propel it forward.

Fontanelli looked at the picture, his eyes widening. His lips trembled for a second, then he lost it completely. "When did she die?" He made no attempt to conceal the emotion in his voice.

Novick nodded. Things weren't going to be as cut and dried as he thought.

"You think she was murdered?"

"I know it," Novick replied.

"Who did it?" Fontanelli seemed genuinely baffled. He was either a better actor than most, or was completely stunned.

"Let me finish my story, Mr. Fontanelli."

Sniffing back a few tears, the businessman said, "Go ahead."

"Ladies in Waiting...the escort service? It belongs to Skylark Enterprises. Mr. Marchibroda told us that. And Skylark? Why, that belongs to Halcyon Corporation. And guess what? That made you Tracy Spillman's boss. Because she was turning tricks for Ladies in Waiting."

"That doesn't necessarily mean she was murdered. I mean—"

"No," Novick interrupted, "that's right, it doesn't. Even buying the farm with a needle in your arm, which is how we found Miss Spillman, doesn't mean that. But when the junk is more than half strychnine...well, what would you think?"

2

The Palermo Social Club looked about as interesting as a derelict grocery store. Its neon sign, with three letters out, winked through the snow, threw weak streams of orange across the narrow street. The simulated brick siding, its black grooves filled with snow, showed its age. The streetlight out front was dim, washing the orange out just a little.

Set in a run-down part of the city, the club attracted little attention. Over the years, other businesses had come and gone. A grocery on the corner was, except for the club, the oldest establishment in the block. Periodically, drawn like moths to a flame, up-and-coming entrepreneurs bought into the promised regeneration of the neighborhood. Invariably they either made a go of it and moved to more prosperous locations or, more likely, the general malaise of the neighborhood did them in. Tucking their tails and a sheaf of bankruptcy applications between their legs, the less fortunate moved on to other pastures.

A narrow alley to the right of the club led to a small asphalt lot in the rear where, at any given time, a half dozen cars could be found. The cars, unexpectedly, tended to be large and new, usually American, although one BMW, in slate-blue metallic flake, was a frequent visitor. To a casual observer, if he noticed at all, the cars seemed to arrive in staggered fashion, unpredictable and random. But the two men watching from across the street knew better.

A slender column of blue-gray smoke coiled up from the club's chimney and disappeared into the blue-gray sky. One of the watchers, now on his third day in the dingy third-floor room, peered through the grimy glass. He watched the smoke for a while, as if it were a lava lamp, losing himself in the unpredictable monotony. He stubbed out a cigarette in a littered ashtray and brushed a few stray ashes from the front of his sweater.

Glancing at his watch, he said, "I don't know about you, Tommy, but I sure as hell am getting tired of this shit detail."

"Relax, Tony. You know how it goes. We hook up the stuff and spend a week or two, then they tell us to tear it down and go someplace else. We'll be out of here in a couple days."

"Not soon enough to suit me." Tony backed away from the window and reached behind him to open the refrigerator door. His hand groped around inside until it closed around a cold bottle. Slamming the door with his hip, he twisted the bottle cap loose and tossed it into the corner, where it clattered into a tin wastebasket. He took a pull on the soda, then looked at the label. "Black cherry, ugh! I hate this job sometimes."

"You rather be out in the snow, my man?"

"Yeah, I think so. At least I could move around a little bit. This is what jail must be like."

"No, it's not, I can tell you. I was under once, in Trenton. Four fucking months, all so I could get next to some dude who got iced before I met him. Complete waste of time that was."

Tommy watched the needles on his VU meters. So far, nothing much was happening. "You know," he said, "I'm beginning to think that the boss is full of shit. You want to know what I think? I think that storeroom is just that. A place full of empties and racks of beer and soda bottles. I haven't heard anything but glass on glass in three days, except for that once. Dumb fuck dropped a case on his foot. Should have heard him. It was in Italian, but I know a blue streak when I hear it."

"What time did you say the Fed was getting here?"

Tommy looked at his watch. "Anytime, now. Supposed to be here at four. Tony, will you relax? You're starting to make me nervous. And I never get nervous. Everybody knows that."

"What the hell do they want, anyhow?"

"Search me. All I know is what Brophy told me. Supposed to be some sort of organized crime penetration thing. I guess they got somebody under. Or plan to, anyhow. I think he must be one of the new faces we saw in the past couple of days. Maybe not. I don't know what the hell is going on."

Feet on the back stairs shut them both up. Tony chugged the rest of the black cherry soda, flipped the bottle into the trash can and adjusted his side arm. He walked toward the back door and heard two sets of feet on the creaky stairs.

Tony opened the door and peered down. A low-wattage bulb, its globe layered in greasy dust, barely lighted the narrow stairwell. On the landing below, he could see two men he didn't recognize. Both were big, but the second man in line was taller than the first.

As they ascended, their bodies gradually filled the stairwell, blocking out the light. It was impossible to see their faces. The man in the lead nodded to Tony and walked past him. He looked around the room with a neutral expression. His face suggested it was no better and no worse than he had expected.

The second man stepped into the room without making a sound. Tony felt cold, as if someone had just opened the downstairs door. But he knew it was the big guy who chilled the room. The silence was thick enough to spread with a trowel.

"Brognola, Department of Justice," the first man announced. "You get anything yet?"

"Nothing," Tommy replied. "Three days of dead air. You bug a tomb, at least you hear the rats."

"You got rats over there, believe it," Brognola said. He turned to his companion. "Looks like you'll be doing some waiting."

"I can handle it."

"You can introduce yourselves later," Brognola continued. "But I want to make one thing perfectly clear. This is a federal op. You don't do anything without my permission. Right now, all I want you to do is listen. You make the tapes, you box them and you ship them out. Clear?"

"Yes, sir," Tommy said. "But Fontanelli probably knows we're here. You can sit on your thumbs till doomsday and not get anything you can use."

"Maybe. Just don't screw it up, that's all. If you blow this, eighteen months of prep goes down the tubes. Any questions?"

"No, sir," Tommy replied.

Brognola looked at Tony as if expecting an argument, but none was forthcoming. The man from

Justice turned to his companion. "You know how to reach me."

The big guy nodded.

Brognola walked to the door and opened it. "I'll be back tomorrow, unless you need me sooner." He left the door open, and they listened to his feet on the creaking stairs.

When the first-floor door banged shut, Tony said, "Unpleasant bastard, isn't he?" He looked at the new arrival, who stared back at him with ice-cold eyes. He said nothing, and Tony started to fidget.

"I guess he knows what he's doing, though," Tony mumbled. "You with Justice?"

"No."

"What then, some detached local?"

"No."

"Talkative, aren't you?"

Mack Bolan ignored him and walked to the window. He bent forward, stopping an inch or two before the dirty pane. The street below was undisturbed, a single set of tire tracks the only mark on three inches of new snow. Mounds of old snow lined the curbs, dirty and yellowing. It showed through here and there, where the wind had stripped the new snow away.

It was almost five o'clock, and the sun had set about a half hour before. The warrior backed away and grabbed a battered wooden chair by the seat, pulling it close to the window. He sat down and hunched forward.

"I guess you know what you're looking for, huh?" Tommy ventured. "You mind clueing us in?"

Before Bolan could answer, the downstairs door creaked. He stood and walked to the head of the stairs, easing the half-open door back just enough to slip through.

"Where you going?" Tony demanded.

Bolan pressed a finger to his lips. He crept halfway up the last flight and pressed himself against the wall. He waved to Tony, indicating that he was to close the door.

Tony did as he was told. He looked at his partner and shrugged. "Bastard is jerking us off, I think. Playing cops and robbers."

"Makes the time go by." Tommy grinned. "We could use a little excitement."

Outside, Bolan tensed. He reached under his jacket for his Desert Eagle and backed another two steps toward the fourth floor. He could hear the whisper of feet on the stairs below, and he knew that it wasn't Brognola. When the big Fed said he'd see you tomorrow, he meant it.

A snap-brimmed hat appeared in the stairwell, quickly followed by a pair of broad shoulders. The newcomer moved quietly, tiptoeing up the stairs and trying each step before letting it bear his weight. Whoever he was, he didn't want anyone to know he was coming. As the guy continued up the stairs, he turned to gesture over his shoulder. Two more men followed him in quick succession, avoiding the same stairs, using the same cautious step.

The Executioner adjusted his grip on the Desert Eagle. In such close quarters, with no cover, three men made for long odds. He hadn't seen a weapon yet, but people didn't creep up back stairs like these guys were unless they were packing. The lead man reached the third floor and stepped aside to let the others fan out. Bolan saw the guns now. Two of the men carried an

Ingram MAC-11; the point man had two automatic pistols. The machine pistols would have to go first. When a man wielded an Ingram, he didn't have to be a marksman at close range, and Bolan couldn't risk a wild spray.

"That's far enough," he said, keeping his voice low so that the men inside wouldn't open the door out of curiosity. "Put the guns on the floor and kick them downstairs."

The two hired hands looked to the point man, who stared up the steps at Bolan. He nodded as if to comply, then dropped to the floor and rolled out of sight.

The Executioner drilled one of the two MAC-toting men, the slug taking him high in the chest. The man flew back into the door, his machine pistol clattering to the floor and bouncing halfway down the steps. A broad smear of blood glistened on the chipped and greasy paint of the door as the gunner slid to the floor.

Before the dropped gun had hit the first step, Bolan had fired again, hitting the second Ingram gunner in the center of the forehead. The man's skull burst like a ripe melon, spewing sticky gray paste and a rain of blood onto the wall behind him.

The big guy dived down the stairs, catching the remaining man off guard. The gunner was just getting to his feet and swung the automatic around.

The door flew open, and Tony fired a quick burst down the empty stairwell without looking. He hollered, "What the hell is going on?" The point man fired twice, just missing Bolan. Hunks of the floor exploded into the air.

The warrior landed on his hip and rolled, getting to his feet in one fluid movement. He fired again. The point man grabbed for his throat and staggered toward Bolan, who stepped aside and gave the guy a shove as he stumbled by.

The careening gunner hit the banister and pitched forward, his head slamming into the far wall as he flipped over. He landed on his head, and the sharp crack of bone echoed in the stairwell. An invisible cloud of cordite swirled in the air, its bite the only vestige of the gunfire.

Tony raced down the stairs after the tumbling body and seemed to reach the landing below at the same time. He bent to pull off the gunner's hat. "Holy shit! That's Larry Gandolfo, a one-man hit squad. What the hell are we into here?"

Tommy appeared in the doorway. "You guys okay?"

When Bolan looked at him, Tommy felt himself shiver. He'd only felt that sensation once before, and that had been in Vietnam, while looking down the barrel of an AK-47.

3

Mack Bolan stared at Tony. "I know who he is. Get inside."

"We can't just leave them there!"

"Let's go." Bolan snared Tony's arm and propelled him into the room.

"You guys keep an eye on the club. I'll handle the rest."

Tommy's mouth had dropped open in amazement. He looked at Bolan, then at the headset sitting on his chair. Without a word he lifted the headphones and fit them into place.

"Hey, we got something."

"Sure you do," Bolan snapped. "You don't think that little raid was a coincidence, do you? They know you're here. But right now, they think you've been taken care of."

"What do you mean, they know? How...?"

"You think about it," Bolan said.

Tommy nodded. Then he held up a finger. "Wait, you got to hear this." He leaned forward and thumbed a toggle. The monitor crackled with a burst of static, then Bolan heard a voice. It sounded distant, hollow, like a man speaking from the bottom of a well.

"Papa," the voice said, "what the hell is going on?"

"You ask me that, Dominick? You dare ask your father something like that? You think I don't know what I'm doing? Is that what you think?"

"I don't know what to think, Papa. You told me we were out of it. You told me it was strictly legitimate from now on. Didn't you?" There was a short pause. Something scraped, and then the voice resumed. "Well, didn't you tell me that?"

"Dominick, I'm telling you to mind your own business. You're a college boy. You have all the degrees, eh? And how do you think you got them? You think I could send you to Harvard on what I made at the fish store? Is that what you think? Dominick, this is not a hobby with me. This is *life*. This is what I am. And what you are."

"No! It's *not* what I am. I'm a businessman, but not that kind of business. I brought you into the company because I wanted you out of that bullshit."

"Don't use that kind of language to me. I'm your father."

"You knew all about it, didn't you."

"What? Knew all about what, Dominick?"

"The escort service. Hookers, Papa, prostitutes. Inside Fontanelli Industries. On the payroll, for Christ's sake."

"Dominick, use your head. Where do you think I got the money to help you start your business? You think I had that in a cookie jar? You think Mama saved it from the grocery money?"

"Where did you get it, then?"

"I have friends, Dominick. You have friends, only you don't know it. They got me the money. They loaned it. At low interest."

"You pay them back?"

"How could I not?"

"How? I see the books. I'd notice something like that."

"Business is where you find it, Dominick. Sometimes, a deal is better than money. One hand washes the other. You feed my dog, I feed yours."

"Don't talk nonsense. Tell me what you did."

"Don't you raise your hand to me. I'm your *father*." The unmistakable sound of a hand striking flesh snapped in the room like an electric discharge. The VU meters leaped to their pegs, then settled back.

"I want to know," Dominick repeated. "Tell me, or so help me, I'll call for an outside audit. You know what that means, don't you? It means the government. Any irregularity, the auditors go straight to Uncle Sam. You want that?"

"Don't stick your hand in a dark hole, Dominick. You might lose it."

"What are you telling me?"

"I shouldn't have to tell you anything. College boy, smart guy. You think you know everything. You don't know *nothing*. Here, college boy, look at this. You see this?"

"What about it? It's a wire, so what?"

"And what do you think is at the end of this wire? Huh?"

"I don't know."

"I'll tell you then. It's a microphone. And where do you think that microphone goes? You think some kid is listening to music somewhere? Let me tell you, the other end of this wire, not ten minutes ago, was in some cop's ear."

"What do you mean, until ten minutes ago? What happened ten minutes ago?"

"Nah, nah, nah, Dominick. Walls have ears, too."

"You mean you hit a cop? Is that what you're telling me?"

The old man said nothing.

"It is, isn't it? That's what you're telling me. Jesus Christ! Some cop came to see me this morning. A homicide cop."

"What about?"

"Do you remember Tracy Spillman? The girl I was engaged to before Roseanne?"

"Trash, that one. No good. Never was."

"She's dead, Papa."

"Good riddance to bad rubbish."

"And do you know where she died? The Laguna Hotel. *Our* Laguna Hotel, as it turns out."

"A good investment."

"You know all about it, don't you?"

"Hotels are good business, Dominick."

"I don't mean that. I mean Tracy. You knew she was dead, didn't you?"

"Trash. She sold herself to anyone. She had no pride."

"She worked for us, did you know that?"

"I knew, yes."

"And you didn't tell me."

"What was I supposed to tell you, that some slut you used to date was peddling her flesh to put money in your pocket? Is that what you wanted me to tell you? And what would you have done if I told you, divorced Roseanne and married her? Dominick, she was no damn good. And she had a big mouth."

"What's that supposed to mean?"

"It means what it means."

"Tell me what the hell you're talking about, dammit. Oh, Christ…you did it, you had her killed, didn't you? You supplied her with the dope. It was easy enough to slip her a doctored hit, wasn't it? You fucking bastard!"

"She was trouble, Dominick. She knew things she had no business knowing. We couldn't take the chance."

"We? Don't try to drag me into this mess."

"I don't have to, Dominick. She did, your Tracy. She dragged you in. I had to drag you out, before you drowned."

Bolan stood listening. The argument waxed and waned, and he seemed transfixed. Twice Tommy made a comment, and twice Bolan hushed him. His eyes were fixed on the spinning reels, as if he could actually see the arguing men.

Not until the sound of a slamming door put an end to the argument did Bolan move. He walked to the window, brushing Tony aside as if he were no more substantial than a curtain. He rubbed at the glass with the tips of his fingers.

The front door of the decrepit club building bounced open, slamming against the wall and bouncing into Dominick Fontanelli as he stepped out.

Bolan watched the tall man head off into the snow. Then he walked to the recorder and clicked it off. Tommy made no move to interfere when the warrior wound the rest of the tape, boxed it and stuck it in his coat pocket.

"Put another tape on," he said, "then call somebody about the mess on the stairs."

Then he was gone.

As Bolan headed down the stairway, he heard Tony say, "What the hell is his story, do you think?"

If Tommy had a guess, Bolan didn't hear it. He stepped into the cold and tugged his coat collar up around his neck. Heading toward the street, he picked up his pace a little. His feet slipped on the snow, and he altered his stride to compensate.

When he reached the street, Fontanelli was no longer in sight. Bolan crossed to the far side, angling away from the Palermo, and picked up Fontanelli's tracks on the pavement. Moving swiftly, he settled into a comfortable gait. He wasn't sure why he was following the man, but instinct told him he should. A square of yellow light splashed on the snow a block away, and he saw a shadow move through it. Fontanelli seemed to be moving with no purpose, more like a man out for a reflective stroll than someone with a destination.

Bolan heard the muffled throb of an engine. The snow dampened the sound, but there was no mistaking the hiss of tires in the crisp snow. He glanced backward, but saw no lights. He was certain the car was in the block behind him. If it had no lights, that could only mean one thing.

The warrior picked up his pace, trying to narrow the gap between Fontanelli and himself. As he reached the corner, a black Buick, its lights out, rolled past, its engine pulsing like a distant dynamo. In the dim light, Bolan couldn't see the occupants, or even whether anyone other than the driver sat in the car.

Fontanelli stopped for a moment, and Bolan caught the glint of a streetlight on bright metal. A second later a small orange flame appeared, then winked out. A small cloud of smoke wreathed Fontanelli's head for a second, then was ripped aside by the wind.

Bolan covered the block in thirty seconds. The Buick sat across from the square of light, just beyond its far edge. A small coil of exhaust was the only evidence that the car was running. When Bolan entered the square, he realized Fontanelli had stepped into a small delicatessen. It was the only place open, as if the town had shut down in anticipation of the storm everyone knew was coming.

Bolan debated whether to enter the store, but decided against it. He didn't want Fontanelli to see him. He continued on past the deli and crossed the street. Behind him, he heard the whir and click of a traffic light changing. A faint green smear on the snow turned amber then, with another whir and click, bright pink.

Stepping onto the curb, Bolan pretended to lose his footing and fell behind a mound of old snow. He was about forty feet past the Buick, and he wormed his way back toward the idling car on his stomach. He heard the whine of an electric window and took a quick look. Fontanelli was framed in the glass door of the deli, about ten feet inside it. If he was aware that he was being watched, he showed no sign.

Bolan squirmed back along the pavement, his breath rasping in his throat. Another ten feet and he was past the Buick. Scrambling to his feet, he ducked between two cars at the curb. He could see shadows in the Buick now, blobs of darkness outlined faintly against the streetlight's glow.

The warrior dropped into a crouch and slipped directly behind the Buick, hoping the driver wasn't looking in his sideview mirror. Holding on to the bumper of the Buick, he hauled himself to the corner of the car, just below the right rear fender. A bell tinkled, and he turned to see Fontanelli pulling the deli door open.

Fontanelli stepped into the doorway, let the door close behind him, drowning out the still-tinkling bell. A gun barrel suddenly appeared in the open front window of the car. Bolan had his own gun in hand and moved toward the window. The barrel protruded farther, and he could see a pair of hands gripping the gun tightly to hold it steady. He lashed out with his foot, and the gun went off with a loud crack. Bolan heard glass breaking, and stuck his Desert Eagle into the car. He fired twice, then was knocked to the ground as the driver stomped on the gas. The Buick's rear wheels spun crazily, and the vehicle yawed to the right. Then its tires caught, and the vehicle swerved away, skidding nearly sideways to the corner. It then gained traction and disappeared.

Bolan hauled himself to his feet and looked toward the deli. The glass in the front door had splintered around an ugly bullet hole. Dominick Fontanelli was gone.

4

"They're already putting the squeeze on him."

"I still don't think we can do anything for him," Brognola protested.

"Hal, if we wait, it'll be too late. I think we have to move now. At least talk to him, see what he says."

"What do you think he's going to say? You think he'll roll over on his own father? Come on, Striker. That's just not in the cards."

"You heard the tape."

"Yeah, I did. I heard it, but I don't know whether I believe it. You don't know that the old man sent those goons. It could have been Dominick."

"And you think he set up the attempted hit on himself, too?"

"I don't know. No, I guess not. That does throw a different light on things."

"Damn right it does."

"What turned you around? Two days ago, you were all gung ho to fry his ass."

"I don't know. There was something about that fight with his father. I think he was genuinely surprised. I think he had no idea what was going on. He even threatened the old man with an audit. Does that sound like a Mob honcho to you?"

"No. But you know that the Mob is changing. These younger guys drive German cars. They talk about marketing niches and diversification. They're all button-down Ivy League types. The young Turks aren't Turks at all, anymore. They're accountants, for God's sake. But they're still killers. That dead girl proves that, doesn't it?"

"I don't know what it proves. All I could tell is that Dominick Fontanelli was surprised and upset when he heard about Tracy Spillman."

"You talk to the homicide cop Dominick mentioned?"

"Not yet, but I'm going to."

"All right then, why don't you talk to him, see what he thinks? Then, if you still feel the same way, talk to Dominick. If he's genuine, I still don't think you're going to get him to roll over. Hell, I'm not even blaming the guy. I'm still enough of an Italian to know how important family is. It just isn't done. Not in this life."

"We'll see." Bolan stood to leave. "I got the name of the homicide guy. Barry Novick. Supposed to be hard-nosed but fair. A good cop, from what I can gather."

"I don't have to tell you not to tell Novick any more than you have to. If we're going to move on this, maybe offer the Witness Protection Program, the fewer people who know about it, the better. It'll take a while to set up. I don't want Fontanelli wasted while the great wheels of the gods do their slow turn."

Bolan walked to the door and paused, his hand on the knob. He turned back to face his friend. "Do me a favor, Hal. Try to find out who knew about the surveillance team. I think there's a leak on the inside. The button men knew exactly where they were going. The timing was perfect. We have our hands full without having to watch our backs. I need to know everything about Fontanelli, father and son. I think the answer might be there in the family history somewhere. Better check out Tracy Spillman, too."

"Anything else?" Brognola asked dryly. "Want me to repaint the White House, too?

A ghost of a smile hovered on Bolan's lips. Then he was gone. Moments later the Executioner climbed into his rented car and keyed the ignition. Novick lived in North Jersey, which was a forty-minute drive with no traffic. Spinning away from the curb, he crossed Foley Square and ignored the lights as he nosed through the dark, quiet streets of lower Manhattan. On the West Side Highway, he could see the Jersey skyline doing its best to emulate the city's own.

Bolan finally took the Bogota exit off I-80. Hitting the small-town streets, he slowed to the posted speed and found Novick's building with no trouble. It was a boxy high rise a mile from the interstate.

The elevator was all simulated wood and smelled of Liquid Gold, as if somebody on the staff couldn't tell the difference between wood and plastic. When the car stopped at twelve, Novick was in the hall. Dressed in jeans and a sweatshirt, he looked as if he'd been sleeping. He smiled easily and took Bolan's outstretched hand. Bolan was surprised at the strength in the smaller man's grip.

"Come on in," Novick said. He waited for Bolan to enter, then said, "Coffee?"

"Black, thanks."

Novick disappeared into a kitchenette, and Bolan heard the practiced rattle of utensils. The detective returned a minute later.

"So, what can I do for you?"

"I wanted to ask you a few questions about Tracy Spillman."

"And about Dominick Fontanelli, right?"

Bolan nodded.

"I can't tell you too much. Not yet, anyway. We're still looking into Spillman's background. With hookers, it's hard to get real detail. It's like paleontology, almost. A bone here, one there. But all the meat is gone. You find this bunch of stuff, brush it off, and try to put it back together. Sometimes the pieces fit, sometimes they don't. Usually, you file the pieces and forget about it. That would have been the thing to do here, except for the Fontanelli business."

"What happened to her, exactly?"

"At first, I thought it was the usual story. A junkie scores some high-grade. Used to the street shit that's been stepped on more times than a rug, she wasn't ready for it, and it killed her. That was at first."

"You said a john called it in."

"Yeah. No big deal, really. The guy was scared. Didn't want his wife to know, or his boss. Seemed more scared of the boss finding out, actually. He thought about running, so he says, but realized he didn't have a prayer. He was registered. If he didn't hang around, we were gonna come looking for him. So he did the 'decent thing,' as he put it. He's clean, as far as I can tell."

"So what do you think happened?"

"Until the ME is done, we won't know for sure, but we already know there was more in that needle than heroin. The john saw it happen. He says he thought she was just shooting up and tried to talk her out of it, but the symptoms aren't right. I think she poisoned

herself. Was poisoned. Don't ask me why or by whom.
Motives I ain't got. Just a gut feeling.''

"How'd you tie her back to Fontanelli?"

"It wasn't easy. She worked for this escort service,
Ladies in Waiting. Fair enough. She was a good-
looking woman, not prime, but close enough. That
put her in the high end of the market. When you follow papers of incorporation, you want to puke.
Fronts, phony names, agents, you name it. All the
blanks are filled in, but the information is garbage.
Still, you find a thread, you pull on it. Sometimes the
sweater comes unraveled. That's what happened
here.''

"That's the business connection. What about the
personal one?"

"That was easy. I talked to a couple of Spillman's
stablemates. They filled me in. Tracy was still moon-
ing over the guy. Years later, can you believe it? I
guess, though, it makes sense. You're down on your
luck, and some guy you used to know is scratching at
the floor of the Fortune Five Hundred, you must ask
yourself 'What if?' a couple times a day, at least.''

"So you went to see him, right?"

"Right. Man, what a place. The building reeks of
success. And Dominick is sitting right on top of it. But
I don't know. Something didn't fit. I wonder if the guy
still had the hots for her. He seemed upset when I told
him.''

"So you don't think he had her killed?"

"To tell you the truth, no, I don't. I can't tell you
why, except maybe his reaction was too real. If he was
acting, he could teach Olivier a few things. No his-
trionics. I've seen all the tricks. After fifteen years,
you know them by heart. And you know what? They

all make the same mistake. They overact. Tears, wailing, gnashing teeth, shaking fists at the heavens. The whole bit. But not this guy. Uh-uh. He was trying to hold it in. Like he was afraid he was going to bawl and was embarrassed. But it got him where he lives. That's for sure. And that tells me he didn't know she was dead until I told him.''

"What else can you tell me about Spillman? You have a motive for anyone else wasting her?''

"Not yet, but I'm working on it. I searched her place, hoping to find something I could use. You know, a notebook maybe, an address book, something with a few leads. Bank accounts, the works. But so far I got zip.''

"Any chance somebody did Spillman to get to Fontanelli?''

"Now that's a tricky angle. I've been thinking about it, but I don't have a hook. I'm not even sure she meant that much to him. I mean, you hear about some girlfriend buying the farm, it could get to you, even if you haven't been close for years. A thing like that, it's like part of yourself dying, you know.''

Bolan knew.

"Let me get the coffee,'' Novick said. He excused himself, and Bolan leaned back in his chair. He knew what Novick was toying with, and he had the same feeling. But there just wasn't anything hard. Like Novick said, there was no hook. Fontanelli himself held the key to that one, if there was a puzzle at all. It could be just what it seemed, could have just been a brief cold whiff of mortality. Fontanelli was, after all, human. It was natural that he would be upset. But there was more to it than that. There had to be.

The curious thing was that Fontanelli suspected his father might have had something to do with Spillman's death. That meant that there was, at least in Dominick Fontanelli's mind, some motive, a hazy one perhaps, but something that made him connect Tracy Spillman's death to his father. Maybe they were barking up the wrong tree. Maybe Novick was looking at the wrong Fontanelli for the link.

Bolan had to talk to the businessman before any of this would make sense. He walked to the door of the kitchenette. "I think I'll pass on the coffee."

Novick nodded. "Okay. You want anything else, let me know. I'll pass along anything I turn up to Brognola."

"Thanks."

5

Bolan parked his car under a clump of snow-cluttered maples. The stiff branches clacked above his head as he climbed out of the car. The quiet reaches of Bergen County were full of estates and lavish private homes, but Dominick Fontanelli had chosen to live in a less prestigious section. The estates were large, and the grounds extensive, but the area spoke more of a desire for solitude than the urge to display wealth.

Unlike most of his neighbors, Fontanelli had opted for land rather than ostentation. The house stood well back from the road, surrounded by 150-year-old pines. A winding drive, lined on both sides by Japanese red maples, leafless in the snow, meandered across the grounds. A simple stone wall, no more than four feet high at its tallest point, was the only obstacle. Bolan approached the wall slowly. It was uncharacteristic of a man who had so much to hide that his home would be relatively accessible as Fontanelli's seemed to be.

Bolan was no stranger to the haunts of the Mafia dons, the lords of organized crime, the drug kingpins. He'd never seen a home so naked to the world as that in which Dominick Fontanelli lived. It was a false note. Or was it? Could Fontanelli be genuine? Bolan wondered. Could he really be what he appeared to be, a successful man who made little of his success, a captain of industry with genuine modesty? As unlikely as that seemed, the Executioner was starting to think it just might be true.

The house wasn't without security—Bolan spotted the video cameras almost immediately. But they were few, and not state of the art. He saw no razor wire, heard no barking Dobermans; broken glass wasn't embedded in the mortar at the top of the wall. Hell, he had seen the homes of dentists with more security than this.

Bolan slipped over the wall. When his feet hit the crusted snow on the far side, he broke into a sprint, dodging from cover to cover, using the clumps of shrubbery, often little more than blue-white mounds under the wind-drifted snow.

The house itself was large, but Bolan had seen larger. The front was glass from corner to corner on the first floor. Facing south, out over landscaped gardens, it had a magnificent view of rolling woodlands beyond the edge of the lawns. If Bolan had to guess, he'd bet some, if not all, of the woods belonged to Fontanelli. Fifty yards from the house, he stopped to get his bearings.

Natural redwood and fieldstone, the place looked like a cover from *Architectural Digest*. Two stories for the most part, with a tall octagonal cupola surrounded by a quasi widow's walk rising another two at one end, the house was dark except for a single window lighted by a dim lamp high in the cupola. Pin spots scattered over the lawns threw a dull glare on the snow, and the reflected light turned the redwood gray.

Bolan debated walking up to the front door and ringing the bell. If Fontanelli was what he seemed to be, he'd be annoyed, but he might answer the door.

On the other hand, if he were what he seemed to be, he might call the police.

It was significant that the man hadn't reported the attempt on his life that evening. That could mean either that he intended to handle the matter in his own way, or that he was too frightened to involve the police. But something about Fontanelli suggested that he wasn't a man who frightened easily.

As the Executioner worked his way toward the rear of the house, he heard a dog bark somewhere inside. But it was the irritated yap of a terrier, not the throaty menace of a guard dog. That, too, was suggestive. Approaching a corner of the house on a line, Bolan worked his way in behind some shrubbery and groped along the wall. His own faint shadow preceded him as he sought a way to get inside.

Scattered Andersen windows, their locks in plain sight and visibly engaged, dotted the side wall. On each, the metallic tape of a conventional burglar alarm gleamed in the reflected light, like a band of tarnished silver. The ground floor was out of the question. The most vulnerable, it was also the most secure. As Bolan turned the corner, intent on finding a way up to the next level of the structure, he heard the telltale click of a hammer being cocked.

"You stop right there, or I'll blow your head off."

Dominick Fontanelli stood in front of Bolan, an unwavering .45 filling his hand.

THE ROOM WAS FULL of smoke. Half a dozen cigars burned in ashtrays or were clutched in thick-knuckled fists. A large oval walnut table occupied the center of a lavishly appointed room. Three Persian rugs were set off by the polished wooden floor. In one corner, a freestanding gun case held six of the finest English shotguns. An antique grandfather clock, its refinished metal gleaming in the indirect light, occupied the opposite corner. A wet bar, its stools neatly aligned, ran a third of the length of the room. Behind it a long mirror, fronted by dozens of whiskey bottles, reflected the ceiling.

Twenty men sat around the table, their voices blending into a buzz of controversy. Everything from the future of the Knicks to the upcoming election was grist for the conversational mill. Not since the pathetically ill-fated Appalachian conference had this many mafia honchos gathered in one place.

One man, though, kept to himself. Sitting alone, at the far end of the table, Guido Fontanelli listened to the racket, but he was unable to concentrate. Even baseball, his passion, didn't engage him. His hands lay on the bright wood like dead things. The arthritic fingers, their joints gnarled like those of an old apple tree, twitched spasmodically. He struggled to keep them under control, but it was a losing battle.

The old man ran one hand through his thatched white hair, then fiddled with his eyebrows. Every hair on his body seemed to tingle, to wriggle like a worm on a hook or writhe like a dying snake. His whole body itched. He rubbed his jaw, and the rasp of a twelve-hour growth against his ancient skin sounded like sandpaper on hard wood.

An arched door at the opposite end of the room quivered. The old man saw the knob turn and the door swung back. Conversation ceased.

A squat man in an impeccable Italian suit stepped into the room, followed by two men who towered above him. The man stood at the far end of the table.

In the utter silence, the tick of an antique clock grew deafening.

The man of the hour waved his hand, palm down. Fontanelli noticed a sapphire ring, encased in liver-spotted flesh. The blue stone caught the light and winked like a star on an expensive Christmas card. The old man sat down, just before his legs gave out altogether.

Still standing, Don Alessandro Carbone surveyed the assembly, pausing a moment at each face, nodding a greeting, moving on to the next. When he got to Guido Fontanelli, a world away at the far end of the table, he shook his head as if a great sadness had just then occurred to him.

"So, everybody's here, no?" Carbone said.

He ignored the mumbled agreement and sat.

"I don't suppose you know why we're here. But I think it best if we hear it from the horse's mouth. That makes sense, doesn't it?"

The shaking heads didn't contradict him. He spread his hands flat on the table. "Since we all agree, I turn the chair over to Guido Fontanelli."

Guido cleared his throat. It felt dry, even sore, and his tongue rubbed at his dry lips. "I'm thirsty," he said. He laughed, but it fell on the table like dry leaves. He knew, as did every man in the room, that this was no laughing matter. He walked to the wet bar and poured himself a glass of water from a crystal pitcher.

Fontanelli took a quick sip, rubbing his lips with the tip of his moistened tongue. Then he downed half the glass and set it on the bar with a crack. He could feel eyes pressing on him, and he wanted to run. But he couldn't. He knew that if he was to walk out of this room now, he could never come back. And this room was where he belonged. This room embodied who and what he was.

He walked back to his chair, nudging it aside with a knee to make room for himself. Leaning forward, he let his spindly arms take his full weight. He had to conceal the shaking of his hands, and this was the only way to do it.

"We, ah, we have a little problem," he began.

"Let us decide how little it is or it isn't," Carbone interrupted. "Just tell us."

Fontanelli nodded. He felt his eyes begin to well, and he closed his lids to squeeze back the water. "We have . . . a problem," he began again.

"Two days ago, a girl . . . a prostitute, died. She, ah, she was an employee of an escort service that we . . . I operate, and . . ." Fontanelli stopped to look at the faces arrayed around the table. He hoped to see some encouragement, some sympathy to help him get through the difficult moments ahead. What he saw instead was blankness. Not a single face betrayed any emotion. The men at the table might have been two dozen statues instead of his colleagues.

"She injected herself with heroin and she died. But it wasn't an overdose. She was poisoned. She . . ." He sensed now that it was getting away from him. Now that he had started to talk, he was losing control of his tongue. The words came tumbling out, and there was nothing he could do to stop them.

"Who did it? Who poisoned her?"

Fontanelli looked down the table to see who had asked the question. Leo Fratello was leaning forward a little, his mouth open. He must have been the one.

"I did."

"Why?" Fratello asked. "And what does this have to do with any of us? You ice some whore, that's your business. It's dumb, but it's your business."

"She, ah, she used to be engaged to my son, Dominick. She came to see me last week. She wanted money. She—"

"Blackmail? What? What the hell are you talking about, Guido?"

"Maybe this is too much for Don Fontanelli," Carbone suggested. "Maybe I should tell you what he told me."

"Maybe somebody should tell somebody something, eh?" Fratello said. "I could be getting my ashes hauled. Instead I'm sitting here listening to some old man babble. I got things to do."

"Things to screw, you mean," Carbone said. The men laughed, but Carbone wasn't smiling.

"What has happened is this. By taking out the whore without authorization, Guido Fontanelli has exposed us to considerable risk. Dominick Fontanelli has threatened to go to the authorities. If that happens, a very valuable enterprise will be compromised, perhaps destroyed. It is an enterprise we have built over the years, with Don Guido's help, naturally." Carbone paused to nod at the old man, but it did nothing to calm him.

"Dominick wouldn't do that," Fratello argued. "I know him. He's a good kid. A little stubborn, maybe, but he knows what's what. He won't do anything."

"We can't afford to take that chance, Leo," Carbone snapped. "We have too much invested. Too much money, and too much time. It would take years to recover our losses."

"So what are you saying? Are you saying we take Dominick out?"

"Do you have another suggestion?"

"Well, no. I mean, I don't know enough details. But there's got to be some other way. I mean, we can't just whack the guy."

"What's the worst-case scenario?"

The questioner was several years younger than most of the men in the room. It was Anthony Califano. Carbone looked at him. The young man seemed out of place here. Slender, longish hair carefully styled and blown dry, Califano was one of the new breed. College educated and impetuous, he had little patience for the old ways, and showed even less respect for the men who tried to keep those ways alive.

Califano smacked his lips in disgust. It was obvious Carbone didn't understand the question. "What I'm asking is this. How much do we stand to lose? If we can cut our losses, maybe we can work around it. Maybe we can make some adjustments. Restructure. No harm, no foul."

"You're like all the other smart asses, Anthony. You don't understand. All you see is money. But there's something more important than money involved here. We are talking about honor. We are talking about respect. Most important, we are talking about the pledge of silence. Without it, we are nothing. You don't see what is happening here. Colombians, Chinese, Japanese. They are all leaning on us. Now, more than ever, we have to stick together. A man who turns his back on his friends doesn't have any friends. And he doesn't deserve to live."

"That's bullshit! That Sicilian mumbo jumbo is a myth. Competence, that's what we ought to talk about. If Don Guido can't handle his business, take it away from him.''

"And if he can't handle his own son? Don't we take him away, too?"

"Whatever." Califano shrugged. "You want to talk dollars and cents, do it. You want to talk this other stuff, you're wasting my time. Times have changed, Don Alessandro. You old men, you always want to hang on to things. You make millions in the rackets, and you sell chickens out of your garage. Don't you understand you can't do both? Don't you understand that you don't *have* to do both? We're legitimate, now. We don't need to run escort services. Whores are trouble. You all know that. Drugs are trouble, too, but they're still profitable. You have to make assessments of the risks involved. How much profit is necessary before a risk is worth taking?''

"The problem with you, Anthony, is that you don't understand that you shouldn't try to change what can't be changed."

"No, not at all. The trouble, Don Alessandro, is that you don't understand that you have to change what *can* be changed. Change or die! It's that simple. You try to hang on to nickels and dimes, chump change. Some woman making a few bucks on her back, who needs it? If you had seen that, none of this would have happened.''

"But it has happened, Anthony. What we have to decide is what to do about it."

"So you want to whack Dominick, as if that isn't the same stupid mistake that got you in deep shit in the first place. Look, Dominick Fontanelli doesn't know anything. Let him go to the cops. What can he tell them? We run an escort service? So, fine. Big deal! We say whoops, sorry, we didn't know. It came with the hotel chain. You walk away from it. No problem."

Fratello cut in. "Look, this isn't the place for this argument. Are we going to do something about Dominick or not?" He glanced at Guido with an apologetic shrug. "If not, let's get out of here. If so, what?"

6

Bolan stood with his hands at half-mast. Dominick Fontanelli cocked his head to one side, like a deer, listening for danger. Waving the pistol, he backed up far enough for Bolan to slip through the doorway.

"Go in backward," Fontanelli ordered.

Bolan had no choice. His heels hit the edge of a thick carpet, and he nearly lost his balance. Fontanelli backed him up another half dozen feet, then followed him through the door. He shifted the pistol to his left hand and reached back to slide the glass door closed with his right.

"Now," Fontanelli said, "who the hell are you? And why were you sneaking around my house?"

"I came to talk to you about Tracy Spillman."

"What about her?" Fontanelli seemed wary all of a sudden. His eyes darted from side to side, as if he didn't want to look at something staring him in the face.

"Suppose you tell me." Now that the initial surprise was past, Bolan was starting to feel more in control. If Fontanelli hadn't killed him yet, the chances were that he wouldn't.

"There's nothing to tell."

"Wrong," Bolan said. "And it isn't what you told your father. You even accused him of being responsible for her death."

Fontanelli looked surprised for an instant, then he smiled. "A bug. You son of a bitch, there was a bug in the storeroom. You must be a cop. You are, aren't you? Then you already know what I know. I told what's his name, Novick, everything."

"No, you didn't. You know it and I know it."

"Then you tell me," Fontanelli cracked. "Why don't you tell me what you want to hear? I can say all right, yes, that's how it was. Then you can get the hell out of here and I can get some sleep."

Fontanelli seemed disturbed, but Bolan couldn't decide how to use it to his advantage. And the man had a gun in his hand. Play it the wrong way and he could get himself killed. But something kept tugging at Bolan's consciousness. There was something in Fontanelli's voice during the argument with his father. Bolan had good instincts. A man didn't last long in Bolan's game without them. And those instincts told him to trust Fontanelli. He didn't know why, and he didn't know how far, but he knew instinctively that the man was a straight shooter.

"You know, Mr. . . . ," Fontanelli began.

"Michael Belasko."

"If I didn't wonder just what the hell you were doing earlier tonight, following me around, you'd be dead right now. Why did you save my life?"

Bolan shrugged. "I don't like back shooters. When they work for the Mob, I like them even less."

"And . . . ?"

"That's all."

"Why don't you sit down?" Fontanelli indicated a leather chair across the room. Bolan glanced at it and took the opportunity to check out the room. It was a large octagon, with a massive fireplace occupying one of the eight sides. A fire snapped behind a metal screen. Two small floor lamps bathed the room in soft light.

A second wall was covered ceiling to floor with bookshelves. The shelves were crammed with books. He was too far away to read the titles of most of them, but history and philosophy seemed to predominate. Fontanelli was getting more and more interesting by the moment. Three or four chairs, two sofas and a small desk comprised the furniture. A brass banker's lamp, shaded in creamy glass, glowed on the desk.

Several framed photographs, arranged in a double arc, hung over the desk. Fontanelli noticed Bolan's gaze. "My museum," he said.

Bolan dropped into the chair. Fontanelli remained standing, the gun still firm in his grip, but the muzzle no longer followed Bolan's every move. Yet there was a vigilance to the man. He was relaxing, but not getting careless.

"I suppose I ought to thank you, but I like to know why people do things. Sometimes you thank somebody for nothing. It turns out they were only helping themselves. When you find out, you feel like a jerk."

"Something tells me you don't have the problem too often."

"Once is too often. Anyway, are you going to tell me what the hell you were doing on my tail, or do I have to guess?"

"Why don't you guess."

Fontanelli shrugged. "Okay. You overheard the argument with my father. You think, hey, this guy is vulnerable. Maybe we can get to him. So, you camp on my ass for a while. As it happens, somebody decides to take a shot at me. Now, you figure you spent all that time following me in the snow, no point in wasting it. I go down, you come up empty, so you interfere. Am I close?"

"Ball park . . ."

"All right, let me tighten it up for you. You hear me and my father argue about Tracy. I say a few things. He gets pissed off, you figure I might be on the money, so maybe I'm pissed enough at the old man I might roll over on him, tell you what I know. Only thing, though, what I told the old man is all I know. You heard it, the whole ball of wax. So, friend, I'm afraid you wasted your time. I appreciate your saving my neck, but that's all she wrote. I got nothing more to say."

Bolan swiveled his head to look at the photos over Fontanelli's desk. He fixed on three showing a much younger Fontanelli in uniform. "Nam?" Bolan asked.

Fontanelli shrugged. "Yeah, two tours—1967 and 1968. But don't ask me any more than that. I don't talk about it. Not to anyone."

"I can understand that."

"You too?"

"Wasn't everybody?"

Fontanelli laughed. "Not really. Maybe that's what was wrong with it. It should have been everybody. Or it should have been nobody at all. But not that way, man. Not that half-assed way. What's wrong with this country, I think, is that we do things ass backward. We ought to draft our politicians and elect our soldiers.

See how much money they spend on the campaign, then."

Bolan grinned. He was starting to like the guy. It was hard not to. He had a no-nonsense approach to things. He was smart, and he had a sense of humor, bitter and sharp-edged, but it was there, and it was on the money. "Let me try this on for size. Hear me out, then tell me what you think. Fair enough?"

Fontanelli nodded.

"For openers, no way you told me, or Barry Novick, everything you know about Tracy Spillman's death. You weren't surprised, but you were shocked. That tells me one thing. It tells me you knew some reason why she *might* get killed. Now, that also tells me that you've seen her, or learned something about her, that was a lot more recent than when you were engaged years ago. How am I doing so far?"

"Go on," Fontanelli said tightly.

"Now here I'm guessing, but I think Tracy Spillman learned something you didn't know, probably by accident. I think she contacted you. I think you didn't believe her, maybe were even a little suspicious. But I think you started to wonder whether maybe she was right. And I think you started looking into the operations of your company. I think you found some things that made you angry. More, even, than Tracy had told you."

"You're pretty wise, aren't you, buddy? Now let's say just for the sake of argument, all right. Hypothetical. You're right, let's say that. What is this mysterious thing I discovered? And what does it have to do with Tracy getting killed?"

"I think you found out that your father was a lot more closely connected with his old friends than you thought. I think you should have looked at things a lot more closely than you did, right from the tip-off, but it's not human nature and nobody can blame you for that. But if you're smart, and a Harvard MBA implies that you are at least of average intelligence, you should have noticed a few things. You didn't because you didn't want to know. You're not stupid, Mr. Fontanelli. That means to me that you ran from the truth. Your father used you. Tracy told you about it, forced you to look at it. Hell, I don't know, maybe she tried to blackmail you. Maybe she warned you out of the goodness of her heart of gold.''

"Don't you talk about her like that, dammit. You don't have the right. You didn't know her."

"That's right, I didn't. Just how well did *you* know her? Lately..."

"That's not your business. That's nobody's business."

"Okay, whatever you say. What was it she told you that has you so upset? It wasn't just prostitution, that much is certain. Hell, that kind of thing hardly raises an eyebrow anymore. So what was it? Was your company being used as a front for running drugs?"

Fontanelli sighed. He turned his back on Bolan, and the gesture spoke volumes. When he answered the question, his voice sounded remote, mechanical, like an automated announcement in the bowels of an airport. "I'm not sure... I think... maybe so. I'm just not sure."

"What have you got so far?"

"Nothing concrete. Look, Fontanelli Industries is a complex structure. Lots of little boxes, one inside another. That's no big deal. Most large corporations are like that. You buy smaller outfits and sometimes they fit, sometimes they don't. When one doesn't fit, you stick it anyplace. You got more important things to do, you'll get to it, but later, not now. So it hangs there, dangling from some dead end on an organizational chart. It's small-time and as the company grows you pay less and less attention. Hell, half the people in the front office don't even know it exists. Usually the worst thing anybody can accuse you of is bad management. But this time...I don't know. I don't think so. Not this time.''

"You know they're not finished with you, don't you? They didn't get you tonight, but it won't be the last time they try."

"Yeah, I know that. But I don't have too many options. I can run and hide, or I can stay and fight. Tough it out. I ran from a fight once in my life, and I swore I'd never do it again."

Bolan shrugged. "Look, this isn't an ordinary fight. You have a family to think about."

"I know that better than you do," Fontanelli snapped. "But I can take care of myself, *and* my family."

"What about Tracy?"

"What about her?"

"Can you take care of that, too? Is that what you're planning, to get even?"

"Maybe."

"Look, Fontanelli, don't be pigheaded. There are ways out of this that you're not considering. The Witness Protection Program..."

Fontanelli snorted. "The Witness Protection Program? You must be joking. Hell, I'd rather hide in Times Square than try that. Do you have any idea how badly that works? Do you?"

"I know there have been problems."

"Then you know why I won't even consider it."

"Okay," Bolan said. "You tell me what you want to do."

"It doesn't concern you."

"I say it does."

"Look, man, I've spent a good part of my life building a business. Maybe I didn't do it right. Maybe I didn't use my head. Maybe I was even willing to look the other way once in a while, ignore things I shouldn't have. But I'm not a crook, and I'm not a coward."

"How can you run the business and protect your family at the same time? You can't run Fontanelli from here, and they can't live in the office. They have lives, too."

"All right, wait a minute, let me think." Fontanelli set the gun on his chair. "I have to think this through."

And Bolan knew he had won.

7

Mack Bolan listened to the two men. His hooded eyes followed the conversation, darting back and forth like those of a spectator at a tennis match. The argument was getting heated. It was the first time in a long while Bolan had seen anyone other than himself keep Brognola off balance. Dominick Fontanelli was a formidable opponent.

"Look, Fontanelli," Brognola was saying, "I can understand your reluctance. It makes you feel like you're running away. But dammit man, that's exactly what you have to do. It's what any prudent man has to do under these circumstances."

"I'm not a prudent man, Mr. Brognola. You don't build an organization like Fontanelli Industries by being prudent. Risk is a part of the game. It's what makes the rewards possible. Hell, it's in all the clichés. You work for the biggest clichémonger on the planet. You ought to respect them. Nothing ventured nothing gained. No pain, no gain."

"And just whose pain are you risking, Fontanelli? Not just yours. You have a family. You think they'll be safe? If these bloodsuckers want you, they'll use your family to get at you. You know it and I know it. You can't just sit there and tell me that doesn't scare you. That it doesn't matter. Because I know it does, and so do you."

"Look, Mr. Brognola. I appreciate what you're saying. I appreciate your concern. I even think it's genuine, and that makes you an extraordinary kind of man in the federal bureaucracy. But I have my pride. I'm a big boy, and I can take care of myself."

"But your sons are eight and ten years old. They *can't*. How about your wife? Can she take care of herself?"

Fontanelli let his head hang like a chastised puppy. "No," he whispered. "No, she can't."

"Well, then?"

"What can you offer me in the way of protection? You don't really understand the way these things work. You have your Witness Protection Program, but it's a joke. In the past few years, many of the protected witnesses have been murdered. Right?"

Brognola nodded. "Right. But—"

"But nothing, Brognola. You can't do it. You can't keep me safe. You can't keep my family safe. Not that way. And if I go into the program, my career is over. I built Fontanelli. All right, I had some help I didn't know about, and it's being used in a way that I don't like and should have known about. I concede that. But now I know. I let it happen, and it's up to me to clean it up. I owe it to myself—and to Tracy."

"Tracy Spillman?" Bolan sat up. This was something new. "Why do you owe it to her?"

"Because she was the one who tipped me. I've been going over the books for weeks. I think I have it figured out, but I still have some work to do."

"Figured what out?" Brognola demanded.

"The gimmick. I think I know what they're doing. When we bought the Translux Hotel chain, we also got three casinos. One in Atlantic City and two in the Caribbean."

"So?"

"It's simple. Casinos are cash businesses, high-volume cash businesses. Perfect for laundering money. The fact that two of them are offshore makes them ideal. We use offshore banks for our casino take. It's easier, and it's all perfectly legal. What they've been doing is running a steady cash flow from the U.S. through the casinos, banking them as casino revenues. It's almost impossible to break from the outside. You have to have access to the nightly receipts at Star Casino in the Bahamas and Fontanelli Palace in Bimini. That narrows the field. There aren't too many men who have access to both, and there's a chance that there's two, one for each casino. But I can figure that out, too. So if you want to do anything, go after the street end. Take down the drug dealers. Leave the business end to me."

"And if they kill you, then what?"

Fontanelli smiled coldly. "If they kill me, you're no worse off than you are now. But if I find what I'm looking for, you're way ahead of the game. How can you turn down a bargain like that?"

Brognola threw up his hands. "I don't know what to think." He looked at Bolan. "What do you think?"

Bolan was silent for several moments, watching Fontanelli thoughtfully. Finally he asked, "Is there someplace we can go? Someplace easier to defend than your home? If we can just cut the odds a little, I think we'll be all right. If that's the price for your cooperation, I think we should pay it. But you have to meet us halfway. Don't tie our hands completely. If you really want to take the bastards down, you have to stay alive. You have the books, and you have access to the corporation computer. Can we set up someplace out of the way?"

Fontanelli shook his head. "I don't know. I have a place in the Sierras, for skiing. It's off the beaten track and it's pretty secure. We could beef it up a little, I suppose."

"Can you do what has to be done there?"

"Yeah, I can."

Bolan looked at Brognola. "It's a compromise."

"All right, all right. I don't like it, but we'll give it a try. On one condition."

"What's that?"

"If there's any sign of trouble we kill the arrangement. Take him in."

Fontanelli grinned. "Fair enough."

"One more thing, Hal."

"What?"

"I want that Jersey cop, Novick. I need at least another man. Can you get him without causing the rumor mill to work overtime?" Bolan looked at Fontanelli. "That all right with you?"

"Yeah. He was okay."

"I'll set it all up," Brognola said, reaching for the telephone.

"THINK CAREFULLY, Mr. Fontanelli. This is important. Is there anyone else you can think of who might be in jeopardy? Anyone in your company? Somebody who might know something he or she shouldn't?"

When Fontanelli spoke, it was as if he were talking to himself. He faced the window, his nose almost pressing against the glass. "I can think of four people. Anthony Califano, my budget director and chief financial officer. He knows more about our finances than I do. A lot more."

"Califano," Bolan said. "Any relation to—"

"He's his son. I know what you're thinking, but Tony is like me. He wanted out and he got out. He's been with me for seven years. I'd trust him with my life. I couldn't have built Fontanelli without him."

"All right," Brognola said, glancing at Bolan, "who else?"

"Peter Cummings. He's the key man in the Bahamas. Oversees the casinos and all our offshore holdings, which are considerable. We're developing some properties there and building a new hotel on St. Martin. He's in charge of that, too."

"Do you trust him, too. With your life?" Bolan asked the question matter-of-factly, without irony, but Fontanelli whirled angrily.

"Look, these men are good men. They are good at what they do, that's why I hired them. But they are also good people. They wouldn't be party to anything like this. Especially not murder."

"Maybe so," Bolan agreed. "But you have to admit one thing, Dominick."

"What's that?"

"If they aren't involved, then someone else is. Someone on the inside."

"What about the other two," Brognola interrupted. "You said there were four."

"Yeah, four. I think Dave Hartford. He's the president of Halcyon, the holding company that oversaw the domestic hotel division, and the escort service. There's also Franklin Jeffries, but I think he's too far out of the chain to make a difference."

"What's he do?"

"He's the corporation's chief accountant. A good man. A bit of an odd duck, but he knows his stuff. In fact, yesterday I asked him to get some papers together for me. Things I wanted to look at, budgets, quarterlies, that kind of stuff. There's got to be some evidence in the papers. There just has to be. But..." He trailed off, baffled and helpless.

"We still have to talk about your father," Brognola reminded him.

"Why?"

"Because he's the first one you went to. Maybe, as you say, you had no clear reason for that. But your gut knew better. You went to see him, and you were angry with him. I want to know why. I think you want to know that, too. Don't you?"

"I already told you. I blamed him. It was his idea to acquire Translux. That's Laguna, now. We changed the name. I just felt like there was something there, that he knew something he should have told me. But I can't prove it. And the more I think about it, the harder it gets to prove. There's just too much chaos. I mean, hell, *I* didn't know what was going on. How can I say that he should have. He's an old man. He knows nothing when it comes to high finance."

"But we're not just talking corporate merger here, Dominick. We're talking about a specific acquisition that was made with your father's help, at his suggestion. And it just so happens that it included a prostitution operation. Something tells me he knew that.

Just like it told you. It's in the gut, Dominick. But the gut knows things the brain can only guess at.''

"I'm telling you—"

"Look, all I ask is that you think about it, okay? Let it cook up here." Brognola tapped his skull with one blunt finger. "If there's anything there, it'll surface. If not, no harm done."

"You're right," Fontanelli said, collapsing into a chair. "You're right."

"Look, I know it's not easy. But it *is* important. In the meantime, I want to pick up Califano, Cummings, Hartford and, what's his name, the other guy?"

"Jeffries."

"Yeah, Jeffries. I think it's better for them if we put them under wraps for a while. But I'll need to get warrants. It's going to take a day or two. I just hope to God that's soon enough."

"Why wouldn't it be?"

"They already tried to take you out. Okay, they blew it, but you're the toughest nut and they know that. If they can put the squeeze on these other guys, they can buy some time."

"All right. Talk to Janice Miller at my office. She'll give you the names and addresses. I'll call her and tell her to cooperate with you."

"I'd appreciate it."

"We have plans to make," Bolan said, sitting down across from Fontanelli. "We'd better get to it."

8

Lassen Airport was barely large enough to handle the Lear jet. After touchdown it rolled into a dilapidated hangar, its engines whining. The pilot was good, and Bolan admired the ease with which the plane maneuvered on the ground. Brognola had vigorously argued against using the Fontanelli plane, but Dominick was adamant. He wanted his family to think this was nothing more than a surprise vacation. Bolan didn't have much faith the fiction would survive more than a day or two, but Fontanelli claimed that the trip itself was the worst part. If Roseanne and the kids found out what was going on later, so be it.

When the jet finally rolled to a stop, the pilot shut the engines down and opened the gangway. Bolan was the first one out of the plane. He motioned to Novick to keep Fontanelli and his family on board.

The hangar was deserted. At this time of year, there was little traffic this high in the mountains. Most of the skiers preferred their mountains a little tamer and their accommodations a little less rustic. If you had to walk a little, that was okay. But to drive over roads that gave even a logging truck a hard time was more than most people wanted to endure.

Bolan headed toward the office. A dim light burned in the small cubicle, but it appeared to be deserted. He stepped through the doorway, pushing the lower half of a Dutch door out of the way with his hip. He heard footsteps on the concrete floor of the hangar, and when he turned, he spotted the pilot ambling toward him.

"I thought I told everyone to stay on the plane," Bolan snapped.

"Yeah, yeah. Look, I got papers to sign, and I got to file a flight plan for the return trip. This is too damn far from civilization to suit me. I get the willies whenever I have to fly out here. Mr. Fontanelli always lets me head back the same day."

"You're going all the way back to the East Coast today?"

"If I can, yeah. Otherwise I stop over in St. Louis, and make the second half first thing in the morning."

"You must be crazy," Bolan said.

"That's what they say. But I'll tell you something, buddy. Ain't nobody crazier than somebody who wants to hang out here. I'd rather go to jail."

Bolan grunted. "Where is everybody?"

"Search me. Louie is usually here. He knew we were coming in. Maybe he's in the head. I'll check." He pushed past Bolan and through a narrow doorway on the other side of the small office. Bolan heard him call Louie a couple of times, then nothing.

The warrior didn't like the feel of things. This wasn't LAX, but it sure as hell shouldn't be a ghost town, either. He called after the pilot, but got no response. He glanced back into the hangar. Novick was sitting on the top step of the gangway. The detective noticed Bolan and waved. Bolan thought about calling him over, but realized it would be better if Novick stayed with the Fontanellis.

A small bell sat on a scarred countertop. When Bolan rapped it sharply with the heel of his hand the tiny tinkle echoed back at him from the room beyond. It was the only sound he heard.

Stepping around the desk, he leaned through the doorway and called to the pilot again. Still no answer. Bolan reached under his coat and pulled the Beretta 93-R from its sling. Weapon held loosely in his hand, he leaned farther through the doorway. An oblong of light, broken by his body, fell on the floor in front of him like a puddle of spilled milk. He stepped all the way through, his head cocked to hear the slightest whisper.

A hand-lettered sign, its paint blurry and smeared at the edges, pointed the way toward the rest rooms. The pilot must have gone that way in his quest for Louie. Bolan followed the sign, his soles grating on the gritty floor. A soft hum filled the narrow passageway, and he found himself leaning against an old-fashioned cooler, the kind on which you lift the lid to fish your drink out of ice-filled water.

A small circular fluorescent light popped and blinked at the far end of the corridor. As Bolan drew closer, he could hear its buzzing and the ping of hot metal as it tried to stay lighted. He smelled something like burning tar, and figured the ballast on the fixture must be gone. The place was small-time heaven.

Another doorway, this one painted half in battleship gray and half in institutional green, spanned the end of the passage. As he drew closer, he saw the door, left ajar, bore another hand-lettered sign, this one in black felt-tip marker on an old shirt cardboard. The sign said Cowboys, and Bolan winced at the certain knowledge that somewhere nearby another sign read Cowgirls. The room beyond was dark.

A familiar stench assaulted Bolan's nostrils as he groped inside the door for a light switch. The wall was sticky and covered with a fine veneer of dust. He found the switch and clicked it on. A bare bulb overhead blinded him momentarily. When his vision cleared, he realized where the smell came from.

On the floor, a chubby man in coveralls lay curled in a ball. A pool of dark blood—already coagulated—glistened on the floor in the alcove formed by his chest and bent knees. One hand was curled around the bone handle of a hunting knife that protruded from his chest. Stitching on the pocket of the coveralls told Bolan that he'd found Louie.

The warrior dropped to one knee and felt for a pulse at Louie's throat. But the man's skin was already cold. The hollow between throat and collarbone was motionless. Louie had been dead for at least two or three hours, possibly even longer.

Bolan straightened and pushed back the stall door. The stall was empty. He listened intently, but only the ping and buzz of the struggling fluorescent light broke the stillness. As he backed out of the men's room, he called to the pilot again. His voice was thunderous in the enclosed space, and from far away, he could hear its echo. It seemed to come from high up, and when he glanced toward the ceiling Bolan saw only bare girders.

He realized they had to get away fast. There might not be a connection between Louie's corpse and Fontanelli's arrival, but he wouldn't want to bet on it.

Bolan sprinted back the way he had come. Novick had left his seat and stood at the bottom of the gangway.

"What's going on?" he hollered.

"I found the manager in the back. He's dead. I don't know where the hell the pilot went, but we have to get out of here."

Dominick Fontanelli stood in the hatchway of the Lear. His lips moved, forming the word "Trouble?"

Bolan nodded. Fontanelli walked down the gangway. "What's happened?" he asked, keeping his voice low.

"The airport manager is dead in the men's room, and your pilot has flown without his plane."

"Shit! I guess Brognola was right."

"Too late to worry about that now. What's the van look like?"

"It's blue and white. A Dodge Caravan. Nevada plates."

"Give me the keys," Bolan said. "I'll get the van. You get the stuff out of the plane. Keep your wife and kids inside until I get here."

Fontanelli dropped the keys into Bolan's outstretched palm. "Listen, Belasko, these guys mean business, don't they?"

"You bet your sweet ass they do."

Fontanelli shook his head as if he couldn't quite believe it. Bolan sprinted out of the yawning mouth of the hangar. A small group of cars, parked nose first against a low stone wall, sat covered in snow at one corner of the hangar, near the office. Bolan spotted the van and raced toward it, the keys jingling in one hand, the Beretta filling the other.

He tried the door of the Caravan, which was open. He started to climb in, then on a hunch, he dropped to one knee and looked under the driver's seat. Like everyone else who trafficked in death, the Mafia had gotten sophisticated in recent years. A pressure switch was no big deal. He could see himself spiraling up through the roof, his legs reduced to hamburger. In the dim light, it was hard to see. He lighted a match and held it close to the seat. In the flickering glow, he could see the seat was clean. He popped the hood release and climbed out to check the engine compartment.

And there it was.

The small bulb under the hood was all he needed to see the dull beige block of plastique. It was crude but effective. Wedged in against the fire wall, it sprouted twin leads from the detonator. The leads were alligator clipped to the terminals of the alternator. Carefully he tugged the detonator free of the explosive, then released the clips. He scooped the plastique out of the well in the fire wall, where it was wedged above the steering column, and tucked it in his pocket. He tossed the detonator into the rear of the van and slammed the hood.

Then he noticed the Buick. The vehicle was parked two cars down from the van, and its hood was clean. In the quiet he could hear the slow drip of melting water. The car hadn't been there long, or it would have cooled to the point that snow no longer melted. Bolan walked to the Buick and touched the hood, which was still warm. He guessed the vehicle hadn't been there more than a half hour. That meant two things. It probably didn't belong to whoever killed Louie, because the car had been used sometime after the murder. And whoever it was, was probably still here.

A chance remained, although a slim one, that the car belonged to someone who had flown out in the last half hour. But Bolan didn't believe that.

Not for a minute.

He hopped into the Caravan and cranked it up. The vehicle bucked as he raced the engine and jerked the automatic transmission into reverse. He spun the wheel and backed into a tight turn, the wheels losing traction on the glazed asphalt. He jerked the lever into drive and raced around the corner of the hangar, flipping the lights on as he headed into the open door. Screeching to a halt under the tail of the Lear, he left the engine running and jumped down to the concrete.

Novick and Fontanelli were walking down the gangway with the last of the luggage. Roseanne Fontanelli was right behind them, a son on each hand. Novick opened the side door of the van and slid it back out of the way. While Roseanne and the boys climbed in, Fontanelli began loading the luggage. Bolan stopped him as he was about to stuff the briefcase into the rear.

"Not that one. That stays in front."

Fontanelli nodded his understanding. "I'll drive," he said.

Novick climbed into the vehicle and tugged the sliding door closed. Bolan heard it click, and jumped into the front passenger seat. Fontanelli loaded the last of the bags, stuffing one between the bucket seats up front and handing another to Novick, who balanced it across his knees.

"Let's go," Bolan said.

Fontanelli climbed in and closed his door. "Seat belts, everybody," he announced. The boys groaned, but complied when their father turned to stare at them.

When the last belt clicked home, Fontanelli spun the wheel and kicked the Caravan into drive. He veered left, to avoid the gangway, and hit the gas as he reached the mouth of the hangar. Bolan opened his briefcase but left the lid over his hands. He found the Desert Eagle and snicked the safety off without removing it from the case. He left his hand on the butt of the big pistol and turned to look through the rear window.

"Dom, what's the hurry?"

"Nothing, Rosie. It's getting dark, that's all. I want to get there before the roads glaze over. They're already too slick for my taste."

"Then maybe you ought to go slower."

"Don't worry about it, okay? Just leave the driving to me."

The hangar fell away behind them, and Bolan squeezed his eyes into a squint, trying to see through the slight glare on the rear window. A sudden spear of light from the cluster of cars by the hangar worried him. He couldn't be sure, but it looked as if the Buick was about to give chase.

He gripped the .44 a little tighter. He had a feeling he was going to need it before too long.

9

The Caravan was sluggish with its heavy load. Fontanelli drove well, but the road wound wildly through the mountains, and he had to ride the brakes. Bolan kept staring back through the rear window, waiting for the Buick. So far he hadn't seen a sign that they were being followed, but in his gut he knew they had been.

Roseanne Fontanelli watched him. In the darkness he couldn't see her features, but he could feel her eyes on his face. Novick tried to engage the kids in conversation, trying everything from sports trivia to knock-knock jokes. But they, like their mother, intuitively sensed the tension. Their response was muted and halfhearted. Novick finally gave up when neither boy laughed at his third elephant joke in a row. He felt, rightly, that a kid who won't be silly had too much on his mind.

"This is one lonely road," Novick said to no one in particular.

"It gets lonelier," Fontanelli answered.

"This the only road to the lodge?"

"The only direct one. You can get there the back way, but that road is a lot worse than this one. You need a 4X4 to handle it, even in good weather."

And then Bolan knew where their pursuit had gone. If luck was on their side, the Buick wouldn't beat them to the lodge. But luck had a way of toying with people, and all indications were that their pursuers were well coordinated. A 4X4 wasn't a scarce commodity in the Sierras. That their pursuers had one did not seem worth arguing about.

"How much further?" Bolan asked.

"Sixteen, eighteen miles. Maybe a little more."

"You seem rather anxious to get there, Mr. Belasko." Roseanne's musical voice took him by surprise.

"Yes, ma'am," he said.

"Do you ski?"

"A little."

"I notice you didn't bring any skis. I was just wondering."

"Roseanne, why don't you relax?" Fontanelli suggested. "You can grill the man later, over dinner."

"I was just making conversation, Dom."

"No, you weren't just making conversation. You were trying to find out why Mr. Belasko is with us. And Mr. Novick, too. Let it be. I'll tell you later."

In the darkness, it wasn't possible to see Roseanne's expression, but Bolan would have bet she wasn't smiling. Fontanelli and his wife had exchanged very few words on the trip, and none of them had been without a sharp edge. If they were having difficulty, it would only complicate matters further.

The van labored up a steep incline, winding through a series of switchbacks. Out the side window, towering firs and lodgepole pines jutted up, their trunks plastered with driven snow. The road itself had been plowed, but a thick layer of compressed snow made the going treacherous.

"They don't worry too much about plowing this high up," Fontanelli said, as if he read Bolan's mind.

"That's all right," Bolan answered. "We weren't counting on much company."

"I get a distinctly opposite impression, Mr. Belasko," Roseanne commented. She seemed almost amused, and Bolan wondered whether she knew more than she let on. It seemed almost as if this elaborate charade, played out principally for her benefit, had been seen through from the very beginning.

"Give it a rest, Rosie." Fontanelli now made no attempt to disguise his irritation.

Roseanne leaned forward and stroked her husband's shoulder. "Aww," she said, "little Dominick is mad at me."

Bolan thought he could smell the smoke. Fontanelli did a slow burn, but held his tongue.

As the vehicle topped a ridge and began the long descent down the other side of the mountain, Bolan spotted two winking lights. They were too small to be headlights, and were spaced too far apart. They winked out as suddenly as they had appeared.

He tapped Fontanelli on the arm. "I saw them," Dominick said.

"You know the area better than I do. What do you think?"

"Boy Scouts hiking?" Novick laughed. "I hope..."

Bolan was worried. The winking lights looked more like a signal than anything else.

Fontanelli was having difficulty controlling the van on the slick surface. He had to fight gravity as well as the slippery road and the impossibly sharp curves. Every hundred yards or so, the van would yaw a little as its balance shifted on a particularly slippery patch.

"Can you handle this road without lights?" Bolan asked.

Fontanelli laughed. "Are you kidding? At this rate of speed, I could handle this road with my eyes closed. What are we doing, fifteen, twenty? Sure..." He depressed a knob, and the headlights went out. The golden glow of the parking lights smeared the glaze ahead of them, giving it the appearance of crushed oranges.

"Parking lights, too."

"You're the boss." Fontanelli shoved the knob all the way in.

Bolan peered ahead, leaning forward, his face almost against the windshield. "Slow a little."

Fontanelli braked, and the red of the taillights splashed around them, reflected off the snow. "No good," Bolan muttered.

Fontanelli stopped and threw the van into park. He kicked on the emergency brake and reached for the map compartment. It popped open, the small bulb impossibly bright in the confines of the van. He grabbed a rolled plastic bag and closed the compartment door. "Wait here," he said. He started to open the door, then reached up and twisted the dome light lens off and removed the bulb. He stuck both in his pocket and opened the door.

Bolan climbed out the passenger door. Fontanelli was already on his knees, working at the screws holding one taillight lens in place. "I don't have time to figure out the fusing," he grunted, "so, we'll just do it this way." When the last screw came out, he popped the lens, removed the bulb and replaced the lens. He repeated the process on the passenger side.

"I gather you think those lights had something to do with us," he said, keeping his voice down.

Bolan shrugged. "Hard to say. But I'm working on that assumption."

"You know, Belasko, you're an interesting guy. You don't miss a trick, and you don't say a goddamn thing you don't have to, do you?"

"Hot air's for balloons."

"Yeah. It is. Look, I'm sorry I was such a pig-headed bastard. You guys know more about this shit than I do. I should have gone along with the program. But it's hard, you know? You think things have changed. You think... Oh, hell. Forget about it."

"We'll be okay."

"I thought I left all this shit in Asia. Killing people I don't know. But I didn't, did I?"

"We'll see." Bolan clapped him on the shoulder. "Let's go."

Back in the van, Fontanelli rapped the steering wheel with his palms. "What now, folks?" His forced good humor fell flat. No one was in the mood for pretending.

"Let's go ahead, see what happens." Bolan's voice was calm, almost ministerial. His matter-of-fact approach made the others realize that whatever they felt or thought, he was no stranger to this kind of situation.

"Someone's trying to—" Roseanne stopped in midsentence. She seemed to catch herself, as if the question had been framed before its significance fully dawned on her. Then, thinking of her sons, she chose to swallow it, knowing that an unasked question still has an answer.

"It'll be all right, Rosie," Fontanelli said, a loving tenderness in the assurance. "It'll be all right."

Bolan removed the Desert Eagle from the briefcase and snapped the case closed. He sat there with the gun in his lap, its bright metal picking up what little light was reflected from the instrument panel. The gun somehow reassured Fontanelli. It seemed like some kind of anchor, something they could use to keep themselves from being swept away. And then he realized it wasn't at all the gun that mattered, but the man who held it. The future of his family rested with a stranger.

"Let's go," Bolan said.

The van began to roll. Fontanelli kept his foot off the gas, working the brake pedal for control. They picked up speed, and the vehicle held steady at fifteen miles an hour. Far below them the lights winked on and off again, then one came on and stayed on.

"Good," Bolan muttered. "They're confused. They don't know where the hell we are. Barry, check behind us. Somebody is being signaled up top. They must have been waiting for us to come over the top. They think they have us pinched."

"They do, don't they?" Novick asked.

"Like hell," Bolan said. "They don't know where we are. They can't squeeze unless they do. Mrs. Fontanelli, get the boys down on the floor, and you stay on top of them."

"But—"

"Do it, Rosie," her husband snapped. "Just do it."

"There's a long straightaway coming up," Fontanelli continued. "If we can—"

"Holy Jesus," Novick shouted.

"What?"

"There's something coming on our tail. It's a monster truck, man."

"Hold on," Fontanelli shouted.

He spun the wheel to the left. The windshield exploded into a thousand splinters, the glass raining over the inside of the van. Bolan ducked instinctively. The shot had passed between him and Fontanelli, who had turned the wheel just in time.

"It's gaining on us," Novick said. Suddenly brilliant light bathed the interior of the van. The onrushing truck had turned on its headlights. "It's about a hundred yards behind us and closing fast."

The van slid into the straightaway, and Fontanelli floored it. He began to pull away from the truck. Novick scrambled over the prostrate woman and children, his gun in his hand. He turned the crank to lower the rear window and dropped to his stomach. On the straightaway, they had more maneuvering room. The road widened to three lanes, to let faster vehicles pass the heavy trucks lumbering up the mountain.

"Can you see the truck?" Novick shouted.

"I got it in the sideview," Fontanelli answered.

"All right, watch it. Slow up a little, let him get closer. A little more...a little more...closer, come on baby, closer...that's it." Novick cooed softly, like a father calming a frightened child. "A little mo..." The rest was drowned out as he emptied his pistol into the truck's windshield. The glass starred and shattered. It hung in its frame in slabs of tenuous fragments, then collapsed into the cab, forced by the wind.

"Got the bastard. I got him."

In his own side mirror, Bolan could see the nose of the truck almost even with their rear bumper. In the glare of the headlights, he couldn't see how much room they had. Or if they had any at all. He leaned out his window and fired twice, taking out both headlights. In the sudden darkness, a thin band of gray-white was visible the length of the truck. They were clear, but just barely.

"Easy on the brake, easy," Bolan cautioned. The truck began to close. Its tractor was abreast of them now, the huge wheels almost as high as the van. Bolan could still see the light between the vehicles. They had maybe four inches of clearance. "Left, Dominick, left a hair. All right, brake slowly now, slowly. Don't yaw, man, don't lose it."

The van slowed imperceptibly, and the truck rushed by. The slipstream shook the van for a moment, and then it was past. Fontanelli nailed the brake and they watched the red lights of the truck's tail recede below them. At the end of the straightaway, the truck plowed straight into the hillside. There was a great plume of snow and then, in a ball of fire, the night split open.

10

Roseanne Fontanelli threw herself on the leather sofa. While the men checked the lodge for security, she sat with her arms crossed, chewing absently at her lower lip. Each time her husband entered, she followed his every move. He seemed to know she was watching him. His shoulders hunched, as if to ward off an assault.

Finally, when he could stand the tension no longer, he sat on the sofa beside her. She pulled her legs up under her to make room. "Are you ready to tell me what's going on?"

Dominick shook his head. "I'm sorry I didn't tell you sooner, but I thought it was best if you didn't worry. I should have known I couldn't keep it from you."

"You've never kept anything from me, Dom. Not that you haven't tried. But I know you too well."

"Not well enough, I'm afraid."

"So tell me. Why are we here? What was that business on the road coming in?" Cocking her head in Novick's direction, she added, "And why are *they* here?"

"Something's happened. I'm not sure exactly what, but it's big, and it's bad."

"How bad?"

"About as bad as it gets."

"Does this have anything to do with your no-good father?"

Fontanelli looked as if she'd slapped him. His head jerked back and his face contorted. It could have been anger, and it could have been pain.

"I'm sorry," she said. "I guess I could have put that better."

"Yes, you're right. On both counts. It does have to do with Papa. And you could have phrased the question less offensively."

"Dom, you're a grown man. Why do you insist on calling him Papa?"

"What else should I call him? He's my father."

"I know. But this isn't Sicily. Even if he doesn't understand that, there's no reason you can't. It sounds silly, a grown man..."

"It's what I've always called him."

"But it sounds like a bad movie. Some horrible Italian soap opera, and he's just as bad. Worse, even. 'Domenico,' for God's sake. Your birth certificate says Dominick. Why in hell can't he?"

Fontanelli slumped back in the sofa. He knew this was going to be difficult. That she was right would not make it any easier. It would help if she would be patient, but it wasn't her long suit.

"So," she said, swiveling on her hips and letting her body conform to his. She dropped her head on his shoulder, and he stroked her hair while he tried to frame his explanation.

"So," he echoed. "Here goes." He tried to make it plain and to keep it short. Unexpectedly she didn't interrupt him. Nor did she groan or interject any of her usual editorials. When he finished, he could have heard a pin drop.

For several minutes neither of them said a word. Dominick listened to the sound of the fire, which popped and crackled. Out of the corner of his eye he could see an occasional shower of sparks when a knot of pitch bubbled and then burst. Off in the distance he heard his sons. They were carrying on as if nothing unusual were hanging over them. The sound of horseplay made him smile a little, and then he felt guilty. Guilty for having been so stupid, and guiltier still for having jeopardized the lives and happiness of the three people in the world who meant the most to him.

Roseanne snuggled more tightly. Silently she took his arms and wrapped them around her, squeezing them against her chest. "Don't let go," she said. "Not for a while."

"I'm scared, too," he said.

"Will we be all right?"

"I think so. It's just for a while. Just until—"

"Don't say anything. Just stay there. We can talk about it later."

Dominick closed his eyes. He felt impossibly tired, and the sound of the fire lulled him. Its warmth made him sleepy. There was more to tell Roseanne, but it could wait. There were more immediate problems to attend to.

Bolan and Novick returned, and Fontanelli got wearily to his feet, leaving Roseanne on the sofa. He thought she'd fallen asleep, but she reached for him. "Where are you going?"

"We have some things to attend to. I'll be back in a bit. Why don't you go up to bed?"

"I'll be with the kids."

He nodded.

When she disappeared at the top of the stairs, Bolan said, "We've checked just about everything. The place seems clean. It's not as secure as I'd like, but we'll have to take care of that in pieces."

"They aren't going to quit, are they? Not until they get me, or you get them?"

"You can answer that better than I can. You know them, and you know just how vulnerable they are. It would help if you could get as much evidence together as you can for Brognola. Once it's in his hands, the odds shift in our favor a little. The pressure's on them. Right now, if they get you, they get it all. And they know it."

"I guess we ought to plan on taking shifts tonight, huh?" Fontanelli asked.

Bolan shook his head. "No, I'd rather you left that to Barry and me. You have other things to do. The sooner you get them done, the sooner we can turn this thing around."

"I'm not helpless, you know," Fontanelli protested. "I'm too tired to crunch numbers tonight, anyway. I have to be sharp. I'm not even sure what I'm looking for, remember."

Bolan understood how the man felt, but he also had a responsibility to protect him. Sometimes a little risk could have a salutary effect. If he made Fontanelli feel helpless, then he would become helpless. That was the last thing they wanted.

"Okay," he said. "Why don't you give me the Cook's tour of the grounds?" He turned to Novick. "Barry, you can handle things here for a while, right?"

Novick grinned. "Hell, yes."

Bolan walked to the foot of the stairs and jerked a leather case from the pile of luggage. He walked back to the table, set the case down and opened it.

Fontanelli whistled. "That's a beauty. A Weatherby Mark V, isn't it? Customized, though."

Bolan didn't answer. He assembled the rifle and slid cartridges into the magazine. He checked the action and made certain the scope was properly aligned. Walking back to the luggage, he knelt and opened a small black footlocker. Fontanelli watched him curiously but couldn't see what he was doing.

When Bolan was finished he straightened, and Fontanelli realized he'd assembled a second weapon.

"Can you handle this?" Bolan handed the other man a rifle.

"An AR-15? In the dark. I carried one of these babies forever." Bolan handed him two clips. Fontanelli stuck one in his pocket and loaded the other. "Let's take a walk." He headed toward the front door.

"Not so fast. You shot recently?"

"Last week. Just clay pigeons, but I still have the eye. Come here, let me show you something." Without waiting to see whether Bolan was behind him, he walked past the stairway and down a hall. He reached to the top of the doorframe, snagged a key and opened the door. He reached in for a light. Bolan heard the click as he stopped just behind Fontanelli. The fluorescent hesitated, flickered twice, blinked on.

Fontanelli stood in the center of the floor and swept his arm in a wide arc. "See this?" he asked. There was no mistaking the pride behind the question. Bolan followed the sweeping arm. One wall featured more than thirty trophies. Bolan nodded appreciatively.

"All mine," Fontanelli said. "And all within the past six years. For a long time, I had no use for guns. But after I got used to the world again, I figured, hell, I had a skill, courtesy of Uncle, so why not get some enjoyment out of it?"

In a case on a second wall, several weapons, each chained in place and all behind thick glass in a locked cabinet, caught Bolan's eye.

"I keep it all in here. The kids...you know how it is. Everything's triple locked. Shooting is a high for me, but part of me thinks it's an addiction, like heroin or coke. I don't know if I could kick if I wanted to. But I figure I'll protect the kids from it if I can. Sort of like smoking outside so the kid doesn't pick up the habit, I guess. Like they don't know. Kids know everything."

Bolan had heard men talk like that about shooting before. Not many men had cordite in the blood, but those who did were incurable. "What did you do in Nam?" he asked.

"LRRPS."

Bolan didn't need to hear anything else. He turned without a word and walked out. Waiting down the hall, he watched as Fontanelli stood in the doorway. His face was more serene than Bolan had ever seen it. Slowly he closed the door.

Back in the main room, Bolan asked Novick to make sure Mrs. Fontanelli kept the curtains closed and used as little light as possible. "And make sure everybody stays away from the windows."

Novick waved as he bounded up the stairs. When he was gone, Bolan walked to the door. He shut all the lights off as he crossed the room, leaving nothing but the dying fire for illumination. He pushed open the door and stepped out into the cold. Fontanelli followed him and locked the door.

The temperature had fallen several degrees since their arrival. The sky had fallen, too—a thick soupy gray swirled overhead. It appeared to be no higher than the treetops, almost as if the tall firs were holding it up.

"Show me around," Bolan whispered as he stepped down into the snow.

Fontanelli led him to the outbuildings. Two guest cottages, each a large single-roomed A-frame, stood about fifty yards from the main house. Both were locked and appeared to be undisturbed. A quick circuit of each showed that the windows were intact and the doors securely fastened with padlocks and hasps. The last outbuilding was a two-story structure that served as a garage on the ground floor and servants' quarters above. This building, too, was unmolested. The Chevy Blazer inside seemed undisturbed. The terrain was less reassuring. Although the lodge was isolated, it wasn't ideally situated from the standpoint of defensibility. Stands of tall trees approached to within twenty or thirty yards in several directions. They offered cover for a clandestine approach, and firing positions for an armed attack. Behind the lodge, the ground sloped up and away toward the top of the mountain nearly a mile off. The terrain was relatively smooth, broken by scattered clumps of trees. In the morning, Bolan was going to have to come back out here and try to minimize the defensive deficits.

Turning back to Fontanelli, he asked, "Do any of the outbuildings connect to the house?"

"Yeah, the garage. There's a tunnel from the basement of the lodge that opens into a small chamber under the garage floor. But it's secure. You can't see it from inside the garage. You have to know it's there. And there are three doors, all of them heavy timber and steel strap hinges. The guy who built this place thought overkill was an interesting concept.''

Fontanelli stood with his back to Bolan. ''You know, I—'' The rest of his words were lost as Bolan hit him just below the knees. The warrior had seen the small red spot of the laser targeting just in time. As Bolan hit the snow, he heard the crack of the rifle somewhere down the hill. He scrambled behind a snowdrift, tugging Fontanelli after him. The executive half crawled and half rolled, then collapsed in a heap, breathing heavily.

The next sound they heard was a vehicle roaring to life and racing away down the snow-covered drive.

11

Bolan jerked the cord and the chain saw buzzed like a runaway motorboat. Shifting his feet, he brought the tongue in close. The chain bit and scattered bark, dusting his feet with sticky particles of wood. The sharp smell of fresh wood swirled around him, mixing with the choking smoke from the saw's gasoline engine. It bothered him to take the tree down, as it had bothered him to take down a dozen others. But they were too close to the house and offered too much cover. They had to go.

The snow had started to fall during the early morning, on Bolan's watch. It continued to snow steadily, but the weather was an advantage. It would hamper attackers on foot, and ordinary vehicular traffic was going to be shut down by the rapid accumulation. Bolan had been in the game too long not to seize any advantage, no matter how unorthodox.

Barry Novick, cursing the luck that had brought him to such an alien world, was patrolling the perimeter they had established. It was essential that they mark and clearly understand the boundaries of an area that must be defended at all cost. To leave such things to chance was to cede control to the enemy. They had already sacrificed too much by taking a defensive posture. Bolan would have preferred taking the fight to the Mob, but it wasn't possible. He had to build something for Fontanelli and Novick to protect, and make it protectable.

Pausing to catch his breath, Bolan looked down the slope toward the lodge. Fontanelli, hampered by the bulletproof vest he wore under a ski jacket, backed the Chevy Blazer toward the lodge, a long length of fresh timber dragging along on the end of a cable. Bolan watched as Fontanelli jumped down from the cab and jerked the winch lever. The log scraped through the snow, but it made no sound that could be heard above the still blaring chain saw in his hands.

Bolan was working on the last tree, and he turned back to start the final cut, slicing down toward the point of a wedge he'd already removed. As the chain chewed its way through the thick trunk, the tree began to creak. Slowly its weight shifted and the fibers grew taut, parting as soon as the teeth came near.

The big fir landed with an impact that shook the ground. On the slope above, some loose snow slipped a bit, like the seed of an avalanche. But it died after failing to collect any additional snow, and tumbled to a halt on a slight rise in the slope.

The tree shifted, rolling a quarter turn to the right. Its jagged stump stuck up out of the snow like a broken bone. Bolan retrieved the saw and lugged it toward the crown of the tree where, one by one, he lopped the branches, dragging each to a pile out of the way. After each one, he shoved at the trunk with a booted foot to make sure the tree still lay stable.

When the last branch had been stripped off, he started on the trunk itself, slicing it into lengths that could be handled by the Blazer. Downing the trees served two purposes. Their removal deprived any would-be attacker of some cover, and the logs could be used to secure the lodge. Fontanelli had been dragging them in place, blocking all but two doors. The trunks were thick enough to stop bullets, and the logs were too heavy to be moved without time and exposure. The idea was to make their removal too risky.

Bolan would have liked to cover the first-floor windows, but that would take more time. And it wouldn't be easy. The gunman with the laser target sight constantly hovered on the edge of Bolan's consciousness. All three men wore bulletproof vests, but they were nothing to pin your hopes on. As tough as Kevlar was, Teflon slugs went through it easily. They might as well have wrapped themselves in cellophane for all the good it would do against that kind of ammunition. And there was, of course, the head shot.

A marksman with a decent scope would go for the kill first time out. The Mob didn't want Fontanelli any way except dead. Taking him alive wasn't a luxury they were likely to pursue. That made the head shot probable. And there was nothing a vest could do about that.

Bolan jerked the saw free after making the last cut. He killed the saw and hung it from the nub of the tree stump, trudged uphill and called to Novick. "I'll take over here. You can give Fontanelli a hand with the rest of the timber."

Novick shuddered dramatically and suppressed a shiver. "Thank God. The wind is fierce up here. I don't like work, but at least it'll warm me up."

"See anything?"

"Nothing. Hell, there's not a sign of life. I haven't even seen a bird. That sniper must have hit and run. You took quite a chance coming back in last night. I would have stayed put." He handed Bolan the Weatherby. "You need a hand, just holler." He fiddled with the earpiece on his com set and jiggled the wire just above his collar. "Damn wire is cold. And it tickles when it moves. I think it must have been easier to be a cop in 1900. Hell, all you needed, at least according to my grandfather, was a nightstick. He used to tell me, 'Barry, in my day, law enforcement was all in the wrists.' He'd mime it, you know? Looked more like a bad Ted Williams impression than any cop I ever saw."

Bolan smiled. "I think he's probably—" He stopped in midsentence and held up a finger.

"What's wrong?" Novick whispered. Bolan shook the finger, and Novick shut up.

"Listen."

Novick cupped his hand around his open ear, then popped the earpiece free to listen with both. "All I hear is the wind, and plenty of it."

Behind them, the Blazer's engine roared, and Bolan raised Fontanelli on the com set. "Shut the engine off, quick."

"What's going—"

"Never mind!" Bolan barked. "Just shut it down."

The engine died. The wind howled, shaking the trees farther up the slope. Slashing snow hissed through the branches, and clumps fell from the quivering limbs. In a sudden quiet, the wind paused to catch its breath, and a faint buzz drifted toward them, as if some strange insect were coming. Then the wind resumed, and it was gone again. Bolan cursed and started up the slope.

Whatever it was, it was coming from the forest high above them. "Get Fontanelli inside," Bolan shouted.

Novick stopped to use the communicator, watching as Fontanelli kicked the Blazer over and swerved toward the garage. As soon as he saw the tiny figure of Fontanelli emerge from the corner of the garage, Novick turned and struggled after Bolan.

The footing was impossible, and Bolan kept slipping. Some of the drifts were waist deep, and the rolling mountainside was full of swoops and rises. The snow hid the irregularities, and anything more than a walk was quickly reduced to a stumble. Bolan pressed on, his breath sawing at his throat. The cold air made his nose burn, and his chest felt as if it were on fire.

The noise was getting closer, now an angry snarl. The warrior passed into a broad arc of lodgepole pines. The snow here was shallower, and he was able to move with less effort. Tugging at the Weatherby, he shrugged its constriction away, adjusting the sling and freeing his arms in his jacket.

Dead ahead, a clump of rocks that were buried to their tips in drifted snow made a natural wall, running across the slope and down at a slight angle. Bolan tumbled in among the boulders, sweat glazing his forehead.

He turned as Novick collapsed behind him. "What is it?" he blurted.

"Small engines, three or four. There just below the crest, off to the left." Bolan pointed with a gloved hand, and Novick craned his neck to see. He was too low to the ground, and struggled into a push-up to see over the tops of the rocks.

"Engines? What has engines out there?"

"You'll see," Bolan grunted, making sure a round was chambered in the Weatherby. He braced himself against the stones, wriggling into a notch between two of the larger boulders. This close to the ridge, the wind was crisp. It whipped the falling snow at a forty-five-degree angle and sucked loose snow off the ground as it swirled through the trees. Visibility was worse than poor.

Bolan scanned the ridge line through the Weatherby's scope, zeroing in on a point that seemed to coincide with the source of the sound. They could hear it now over the wind, an angry oscillation as the snowmobiles jounced over the undulating ground. Alternately straining and racing, the vehicles began to be individually distinguishable. There were three of them, Bolan was certain.

The prow of the first snowmobile popped over the ridge, its blunt nose like that of a breaching whale. It left the ground, its engine rising to a high-pitched whine, then growling as it hit on the down slope and its treads bit into the snow. In quick succession two more—one on either side of the first—roared into view. The point sled swung in a tight circle, waiting for the others to catch up.

"Jesus Christ!" Novick muttered. "Just what we need."

Each sled carried a man wearing a ski mask and heavy jacket. Each had an automatic rifle slung over his shoulder. Bolan sighed. At least he didn't have to worry about innocent people accidentally gone astray. The three men clearly meant business—and there could be no doubt about the nature of that business.

The three snowmobiles huddled together, their engines muttering impatiently as the riders conferred. The point man, wearing a blue ski mask, pointed toward the lodge far below. Bolan turned to see the feathery plume of dark black smoke, barely visible through the driving snow. From this angle, the lodge itself was little more than a random assortment of lines and angles.

He wondered whether this might just be one contingent of a multisided attack. It occurred to him to send Novick down, but that would expose him to their guns and betray his own presence. "Get Fontanelli on the radio. Tell him what's happening and to keep a sharp lookout."

"What are you going to do?"

"What do you think?" Bolan raised the Weatherby to his shoulder.

No sooner had he drawn a bead on the point man than the snowmobiles lurched forward. Bolan tracked the leader in his sight and squeezed the trigger. The slug found its mark, a bright spray of blood splattering the white tail of the sled. The point man pitched sideways into the snow. His sled, suddenly free of its burden, careened in a circle, slowly working its way downhill. The engine, without a foot on the accelerator, fell to a slow idle. The sled whirled until it came to rest, nose first, against a tree.

The remaining two men were stunned initially, but one, a man in a green ski mask, pointed toward the jumbled rocks and unslung his M-16.

He cut loose with a burst that chewed at the tops of the boulders, scattering chips of rock and sparks in every direction. Bolan ducked below the fire and rolled to his right. By the time he got a clear shot, the third gunner, in a red ski mask, had swung around. He sped straight toward the rocks, his own M-16 bouncing as he tried to steady it on top of the Plexiglas windscreen. The guy squeezed off a burst.

Bolan could see the red mask through the scope, just behind the windscreen. The cloudy plastic reduced it to a blur. The Weatherby's bite ripped through the screen.

Bolan rolled back to the boulders as the snowmobile raced into a stand of Douglas firs. An angry whine bored in under a full head of steam, and Bolan hugged the snow, dragging the oblivious Novick down against the base of the rocks. The whine became a snarl as the sled homed in, then rose high overhead, like some weird daredevil trying to jump a dozen cars. The driver, dislodged by the sudden jolt, fell backward off the sled. His head slammed into Novick's ribs, then the corpse rolled over several times, trailing blood and gore behind it.

Novick moaned as he wiped at the blood and brains in his lap, then lost his lunch. Bolan leaped to his feet as the third snowmobile spun around. It made a dash out of the trees, and the driver, doubled over like a kid on his first two-wheeler, was leaning on the gas. Bolan drew a bead. Just as he squeezed, the driver jerked the wheel and the shot went wide, puncturing the fuel line. Almost instantly, flaming gas streamed along the side of the sled. The driver slapped at his legs and tried to throw himself free.

The tank exploded with a thunderclap, spewing liquid hell in every direction. The driver, thrown free by the blast, tumbled through the gray air like a ball of lightning. The snowmobile disappeared into the snow.

In the sudden quiet, Bolan could hear only the hiss of snow melting under the flames.

12

Anthony Califano parked his car in the semicircular driveway in front of his home. He climbed out of the silver BMW 320i and locked it. Even in Katonah you had to be careful. Things were getting out of hand all over the place. If you pay two million dollars for a house, you should be able to leave your car unlocked in your driveway. Califano stood looking at the car in the fading light. The windshield picked up a hint of the dark pink and purple as the sun began to set.

The house was on a hill above him. Stone steps, hand-cut and carefully assembled, bridged the fifteen-foot gap. His wife, Ellen, didn't like the idea of climbing steps in the winter, but he liked the house, and he liked the seclusion. Wrapped in trees on three sides, and separated from the street by a steep lawn and a tall hedge, even in winter you could believe you didn't have neighbors for ten miles.

Califano moistened a finger and scraped at a small spot on the BMW's roof. It was sticky, like a berry or a bug had gotten squashed on it. When the roof was clean, he looked up at the house. In the third-floor windows, he could see a reflection of the sun, now no more than a scarlet parenthesis lying on its side.

It got dark all at once, as if someone had turned off a light. Califano started for the stairs. A blocky shadow suddenly appeared on the first landing, ten feet above him. It moved toward him, and he backed off the stairwell. "Who the hell are you?" Califano barked.

"Relax, Tony. Relax. It's me, Petey."

"Dammit, Pete, you startled me."

"Scared you, too, didn't I?

"What the hell do you think startled means?"

"Hey, I don't know. But I know from scared. Scared means you shit your pants. That what startled means, too?"

"What are you doing here, anyway?"

"Like I said, relax. We got some business."

Pete DiFalco bounced down the steps, a pair of leather gloves in one hand. He had the other hand in the pocket of his overcoat. When he reached the bottom step and dropped to the asphalt driveway, he sat on the second step, carefully tucking his coat under him.

"You want something particular?" Califano was starting to get nervous. He heard his voice crack, and it sounded tinny to his own ears, strained.

DiFalco didn't answer. Instead he took the other hand out of his coat and started slapping the naked palm with his gloves. The steady smack-smack-smack of the leather on skin was unnerving.

"Quit that, would you?" Califano snapped.

"Relax, Tony. You're too much on edge, man. You need to get more pussy, huh? Something to relieve the tension. You're working too hard, maybe."

Califano was about to answer when a car swung through the opening in the hedge below them. The driveway wound up through rhododendrons, and the shrubs fragmented the headlights of the approaching car. "It's about time," DiFalco muttered.

"Who's that?"

"Billy. Don't worry about it. Hey, Tone, lighten up, man."

"What the hell is going on? Why are you here?"

"We got a job, all right? We got a fucking job. And Carbone wants you to come along, make sure we don't fuck it up."

"Why didn't he tell me?"

"Hey, you ask him. Maybe he figured he told me, and if I tell you, he saves a quarter, you know? Maybe not, though. Maybe not. We'll ask him later, okay?"

The car stopped behind Califano's BMW. The driver climbed out but left the headlights on and the engine running. Billy DiFalco walked toward the two men. "You guys ready, or what?"

"We got time, Billy. We got time. I was just telling Tony here that he should ask Carbone why he's so cheap with the phone calls. He was asking me and I tell him I don't know, he should take it up with the man himself. Better yet, he should fucking forget about it."

"You tell him that?"

"No. I just thought of it now. The main thing is, we're here."

"Okay, let's go, then." Billy turned and walked back to the car. Pete took Califano's arm and pulled him gently. "Come on, man," he said. "We got a schedule to keep, you know?"

"Hang on. Let me just run up and tell Ellen I'll be out for a while."

"Hey, do you have to clear everything you do with the little woman, or what? College make you pussy-whipped, Tony? You didn't used to be like that."

Califano shrugged. "How long are we going to be?"

"Hey, I dunno. An hour or two. Probably no more. Why?"

"Let's go, then."

Pete opened the back door for Califano, then slid into the front seat beside his brother. The car squeezed past the BMW, then swung back down the driveway.

"Where we going?"

"Hackensack. Tony B.'s place."

"The warehouse?"

"Yeah, the warehouse."

"What for?"

"We got somebody we need to know things from. You're the man to ask the fucking questions."

"Who?"

"Hey, Tony, you don't like surprises, or what? Where's your sense of fun?"

"All right, all right. I just thought, you know, you tell me what you need to know, I can figure out the questions."

"An Einstein like you? Shit, you don't need time. This is a piece of cake. Forget about it."

On the outskirts of Hackensack, the car nosed into a deserted parking lot. At the rear of the parking lot, well off the road, a Quonset-style structure bore the legend Tony Baldassare Moving and Storage. The car eased around the edge of the building, bouncing in some potholes, and took another corner. Billy Di-Falco parked behind the building and shut off the engine.

Califano climbed out of the car. Off to the east, the New York skyline, brilliantly colored against the jet-black sky, stretched from north to south, fading away toward Westchester and vanishing abruptly just past the twin towers of the World Trade Center.

In the foreground, marsh grass and swamp water, both covered with snow, except where the river meandered through the marshlands, provided the perfect foil for the city's extravagance. In the middle distance, an old steam engine, puffing perfect clouds like the old Lucky Strike sign in Times Square, chuffed toward the city, tugging a long string of empty boxcars. The wheels clattered on the rails, and while Tony stared at the peculiar spectacle, the engine let out a mournful wail that drifted into the distance, echoing off the warehouse walls towering behind him and the cluster of boulders on the broken face of a hill just to the north.

"Always hated that fucking noise," Billy said. "It gives me the goddamn creeps."

Pete opened the door and held it for Tony and his brother. Once inside, he let it slam shut. The door banged into its frame, rattling the small wired window in its center and sending an echo through the cavernous interior. Far across the nearly empty floor, a small light burned over a glass-and-steel cubicle that doubled as office and men's room. Billy led the way.

As they drew closer, Califano saw a shadow on the frosted glass. Billy DiFalco called hello, and a door opened on the cubicle. The shadow was still there, and Califano figured there were at least two men inside. He was baffled by the strange summons, and his nervousness returned. When they reached the cubicle, Billy entered first. The man in the doorway stepped back to admit him, and Califano recognized Fred Merzetti.

Califano suppressed an involuntary shiver. Merzetti was known as Freddy Kilowatt, because of his penchant for using electricity to torture people who ran afoul of Carbone.

"Freddy, how's it hanging, Bud?" Billy asked. Merzetti grunted and waved impatiently for Califano and Pete to step inside. He slammed the door behind them.

In the corner, facing the wall, a man was strapped to a chair with three leather belts. A pool of water surrounded a drain in the floor near his feet. A pipe protruded five or six inches from the drain, and copper wire coiled around the pipe and snaked across the pool, where it wound around the restrained man's bare leg.

"Son of a bitch says he don't know what I'm askin' him," Merzetti complained. "Maybe you guys can do better."

"Take off your coat, Tony," Pete said. "You got work to do."

Califano removed his top coat, and Pete thrust him forward. Merzetti stood in the corner, a set of jumper cables in his hand. A truck battery on the floor behind him was attached to the other end of the cables. Califano stumbled and fell to the floor. When he regained his feet, he saw the prisoner's face for the first time.

"Jesus Christ, Dave, what the—"

Dave Hartford, his mouth stuffed with a dirty rag and sealed with silver gaffer's tape, looked terrified. His face was a mass of bruises. Angry welts ran down both sides of his chest, and blisters covered the rest of his skin from collarbone to navel. His genitals were red and blistered as well.

"You ready to talk?" Merzetti demanded.

Hartford nodded, and his torturer leaned forward to strip the tape away. Hartford nearly gagged on the dirty rag as Merzetti tugged it free. He moaned, and it was like no sound Califano had ever heard.

"He's all yours, Tony," Merzetti said.

"All mine for what? I don't know what the fuck I'm even doing here. What am I supposed to ask him?" Califano turned to Billy DiFalco, a helpless look on his face.

"My God, is all this necessary?" Califano asked.

"Weak stomach, Tony? No, it ain't necessary. Fucker tells us what we want to know, it ain't. It's up to him."

"What *do* you want to know?"

"Nothing much. Just what he told Dominick Fontanelli about the casino receipts."

"And did you ask him that?"

"Hell yes! Son of a bitch says he didn't say nothing."

"Maybe he's telling the truth."

"Yeah, and maybe I'm the queen of England."

Califano knelt by Hartford's chair. "Dave, can you hear me? Can you understand me?"

Hartford moaned, but his head nodded. Tony's stomach churned at the smell of blistered flesh. But if Hartford was going to survive this, he had better give them what they wanted.

"Did you discuss anything about the cash deposits with Dominick?"

Hartford shook his head vigorously. His cracked and bleeding lips were unable to produce an intelligible sound.

"What about the accounts? Not the deposits, the accounts themselves, in Grand Cay International. Did you discuss them?"

Hartford nodded.

"What did you tell him?"

"Bawaanz and stemunz. Thaz aww."

"Are you sure?"

Again, a nod.

Califano straightened up. "Jesus Christ. I don't understand you guys. I really don't."

"What did he say?"

"He said he discussed the balance and the monthly statements. That's all. Nothing about where the money came from or where it went."

"How do we know that? Fucking guy would say anything to get off the juice." Billy DiFalco sounded skeptical.

"Sure he would. So would you. So would I. But what's the point? You torture the guy, he'll keep on trying to tell you what you want to hear. Once you go that far, how the hell do you know what to believe?"

"All right, all right. You believe him?"

"Yeah, I do. Can we go now?"

"Sure, we can go now, Tony. Where you want to go?"

Billy DiFalco sounded odd, and Califano turned around just in time to dodge the full force of the sledgehammer. It glanced off his temple and broke his collarbone. He fell to the floor, holding the injured shoulder. He looked up as a shadow passed over him. The sledge caught him flush this time, crushing the front of his skull and sending a hundred slivers of bone back into the brain.

"Should have let me have the conceited fucker."

"What for, Freddy? You want to cook his balls and eat 'em? You already got one set." Billy turned to his brother. "Petey, get the fucking saw. We got to get both these guys in just three barrels."

His brother grunted. Billy walked over to the chair and took Hartford's head in both hands. He gave a quick jerk and Hartford's neck snapped with a sound like a tree limb breaking.

"Better luck next time, you brutal bastard," he said to Merzetti.

13

The lodge was pitch-black. Dominick Fontanelli sat on the sofa, staring at the ruins of the fire. A dozen bright coals stared back at him, like unforgiving eyes. The last log, blackened into charcoal, cracked and fell from the andirons, scattering stars in every direction. It seemed to Dominick as if he were looking at the ruins of his own life.

The drink at his elbow, his fourth double of the night, was almost empty. The ice in the bottom of the glass shifted as if in sympathy with the ruined log. The night was quiet, except for the wind outside, which howled around the acute angles of the roof, growling at the corners of the building as if it wanted to get inside to get at him. The clattering of the cubes was like the gnashing of hungry teeth as he hoisted the glass and drained it.

Everybody had always wanted a piece of Dominick, as long as he could remember. And he had a long memory. Closing his eyes and leaning back against the soft leather, he could see it all, like snapshots in a photo album.

Little Italy, that teeming hive of old men and older ways, swam before his liquorish eyes, and he could see himself walking its tangled streets. It all seemed so real, so present, so overwhelming. His nostrils twitched at the memory of Sciavone's bakery, where he worked after school. He remembered, too, Angelo Fraboni, who paid weekly visits to the bakery. It was always the same thing. Fraboni came in and asked for his box of cannoli. Carmine Sciavone always refused to let Dominick fill the order. He didn't know what was so special about the order until two years later, when Carmine died and his wife took over the business.

Fraboni came in the Friday after the funeral and asked for the same thing, always four cannoli, always in a box. He stood there, a smirk on his thick-featured face, watching the old woman fold the box and slip the cardboard tongues in place. Four cannoli, each in its own sheet of wax paper, snatched from a box on the countertop, like Kleenex. He could still hear the snap of the string as Mrs. Sciavone curled her chubby fingers around it, tugged it free and began to tie the box.

Dominick didn't know why, but he stood just inside the back room, watching as if he were in a theater. When she tied a double bow in the string, Fraboni stood there with his mouth curled into an amazed sneer.

"What the fuck is that?" he asked, as she shoved the box across the glass countertop. "You a comedian, or what?"

Mrs. Sciavone looked confused. "Cannoli. You wanted four, no?"

"No, I don't want no fucking cannoli."

"But—"

"But my ass. Where's the money? You didn't put no money in the box."

"Money? I don't know what you mean. I—"

"Don't give me that shit." Fraboni picked up the box and hurled it against the front window. The impact snapped the string and burst the fragile carton. Streaks of the cream filling oozed down the glass.

Then Fraboni leaned over the counter and slapped her. The blow drew blood from the woman's lip, and she stumbled into the bread rack behind her. Mrs. Sciavone seemed stunned. Dominick thought she was going to cry, but she didn't make a sound. She just stood there, trembling. He thought he had to do something, but he didn't know what. He was fifteen years old. He walked out of the back room, and Fraboni glared at him.

"Hey, what the fuck do you want?"

"I work here. You know that, I was just—"

"Don't tell me what I know. I know what I know. Go in the back and stay there."

"But—"

Fraboni punched him. Dominick fell back, hitting his head on the glass. As he lost consciousness, he heard the bell over the front door tinkle. When he came to, Fraboni was gone, and Mrs. Sciavone held a cold cloth to his forehead.

Mrs. Sciavone closed the shop early and walked him home. At dinner he explained the black eye and cut on his lip. He remembered the look on his father's face when he told about the cannoli. He'd seen the look before, but had never known what it meant. He didn't know then, either. The look stayed there for four days.

On the fifth day, they found Angelo Fraboni in a trash barrel, floating in the East River. People who could talk about nothing but the incident at the bakery were suddenly interested in sports. Nobody mentioned Angelo Fraboni. But the look on his father's face had disappeared.

And that's when he knew.

He asked his father about it, but the old man just said "Widows deserve respect." End of discussion.

"Rispetto," Dominick whispered in the darkness of the lodge. He squeezed the glass until it cracked in his hand. He thought about throwing it into the fire, in some sort of ritual cleansing, but knew it wouldn't work. It wouldn't change anything. It wouldn't bring back Tracy Spillman.

He remembered the first time he'd seen her. The only Jewish girl in his neighborhood, she had few friends and many suitors. Possessed of a beauty that was almost ethereal and, alongside the Italian girls, exotic, she was the subject of rumors and jokes whispered behind closed fingers.

Dominick fell for her in a big way. But her father had no use for Italians, no more use, in fact, than his own father had for Jews. Against all odds—and family pressure—they dated for a year and a half. Dominick was eighteen when Tracy went, was sent actually, away to college in Chicago. His father insisted he go to Harvard and he refused. He went to Chicago to be with Tracy, but the draft caught up with him in two months.

The draft, he thought, a perfect name for it. Even now, he felt a cold wind on his neck when he thought of it. And a colder wind when he thought of what the Army made of him. Her letters were infrequent; his almost daily. Then she stopped writing altogether, and that's when he turned, in a carefully considered, elaborate notion of self-destruction, to the LRRPS.

Uncivilized, almost feral, he roamed the jungle for weeks on end, seeing few faces, yellow or white. The war changed him, scraping away his insides until he literally believed he was hollow inside, a balloon of skin on a bone frame. Everything human in him was gone.

He started writing letters to Tracy from the jungle, leaving one on each Cong that he nailed, like a calling card. The letters got longer, and he got more crazed. Long, rambling streams of consciousness, scratched on rice paper with stolen pens, they were the only vestige of whatever he had been.

The hallucinations started, and he saw Tracy in those rare clouds whenever the canopy thinned and he could see the sky. He took to climbing trees, up where the parrots and monkeys were, strapping himself to a limb and sleeping for twenty-four hours straight. And then the frenzy would come and he would scuttle down the tree, as unused to civilization as the first man, and go on a rampage.

The lack of discipline suited Dominick. He was unfit for companionship, let alone authority, and he knew it. He dived so deeply into the murky water of his resentment, that he had come out the bottom of the abyss into another world. The rage was gone. The blood lust, either sated or transformed, was also gone. He went back in and found that his last tour had expired two months earlier.

He went home and left Tracy Spillman in the jungle. Or so he thought.

Harvard for college, then an MBA, gave him some stability. And look at just how fucking stable I am, he thought. He got up, almost losing his balance, and walked to the bar to mix himself another drink. He groped in the ice bucket for a handful of cubes, then filled the glass with bourbon. He staggered back to the sofa and collapsed onto the leather. His drink sloshed over the rim of the glass and soaked his lap. The smell of bourbon swirled around him and he took a long pull, choking off the urge to vomit.

He remembered the last time he saw Tracy. Prowling the streets of Greenwich Village, already beginning to sculpt Fontanelli Industries with a loan his father arranged for him, he had spotted her coming out of a nightclub. She was joking with two other women. He thought for a moment he was hallucinating. But when she turned, and her face went blank, he knew it was Tracy.

Dominick took her by the elbow and dragged her off. He remembered how she waved over his shoulder at her friends. And for three months he saw her every night. They made love for the first time that night, and every word of every letter came pouring out of him. He battered her as if he wanted her to suffer for all those months in the jungle, months without a word, endless months when he thought of nothing but her, and she thought of anything but him.

He never asked why she'd stopped writing, and she never told him. Then one night he showed up at her place without calling. Tracy wasn't alone. Peering at him around the chain lock, speechless, her face frozen in wide-eyed surprise, she had tried to close the door. But he shoved it open, snapping the chain.

A fat guy with a wrinkled belly came out of the bedroom. He wore garters to hold up his socks, and boxer shorts. He looked frightened. "You a cop?" he'd asked. And then Dominick knew.

"Tracy, why?" he asked, and she shook her head, still speechless. Even now, he could see the room as he backed toward the door, the way parts of her life floated into view at the edge of his vision. By the time he stood in the doorway, he could see it all. He could see it all, and he understood none of it.

Tracy walked to the door, gave him a wan smile and closed it in his face. He stood there for several seconds.

"Who the fuck was that?" the fat guy asked.

Fontanelli had waited for her answer. When it came he turned and walked away. "Just somebody I used to know."

He said it aloud now, softly. "Just somebody I used to know."

And now that's all that Tracy was. Somebody he used to know, somebody dead.

But he wanted to know who killed her. It seemed as if he'd lost her twice, and neither time was his fault. It didn't seem fair. He felt that he owed her something, at least the satisfaction of knowing that the man or men responsible for her death were themselves rendered nonexistent. Dead. He owed it to her.

Dominick tossed off the last of his drink and stumbled off to bed.

14

"Dom, Anthony is having trouble breathing." Rose-anne Fontanelli stood in the doorway wringing her hands. Her husband looked up from the computer terminal as if he hadn't heard.

"Dom, did you hear me?"

"Yeah, I heard you. Did you give him his medicine?"

"Yes. Everything. It's not doing any good. I think he's getting worse."

"Okay, I'll come take a look. Be there in a minute." To Bolan he said, "Keep an eye on the screen, will you? I've asked it to search for a half dozen items. When that number stops changing, it'll mean it found the first one. Come get me."

Bolan nodded.

Fontanelli stepped quickly after his wife. She stood waiting at the top of the stairs. "It took you long enough."

"Don't start, Rosie. I have important things to do."

"And I suppose your son's health isn't important."

"I didn't say that, and you know better. But you baby him too much. Every time he sneezes, you want to run for the emergency room."

"Well, it's not my fault he has asthma. It's in your family, not mine."

Fontanelli winced. He'd felt the guilt ever since the disease was first diagnosed, but Roseanne found it a convenient tool, and she used it like a master mechanic. He was convinced that half of Anthony's attacks were in Roseanne's mind, and half of the rest weren't nearly as severe as she made out. Asthma was no joke, and he didn't take it lightly. But he felt as if he had to compensate for her overreaction. The only way to do that was to downplay it, especially in front of Anthony, who was too sensitive by half, and who hung on his mother's every word.

Ducking into the boys' bedroom, he found Anthony lying under a blanket. His feet stuck out from the bottom, his Air Jordans untied but still on.

"Trouble, sport?" he asked, tousling his son's hair. The boy nodded.

"Hard to breathe, huh?"

"Yeah."

"Let me listen." Fontanelli fell to one knee and pulled the blanket away. Tugging Anthony's shirt up around his neck, he placed his head on the boy's chest. The congestion was evident, and every breath sounded as if it was being forced through a thick mucus. Anthony coughed, and his breathing got more labored. This was no figment of Roseanne's imagination.

Fontanelli sat on the edge of the bed and spread his hand over the boy's rib cage. The muscles twitched, and the chest rose and fell as if Anthony had just finished a heavy workout. In a way, he was in the middle of one. The steady whistle of the boy's wheezing filled the room. He looked pale, except where his skin was flushed along the jawline. That was one of the incontrovertible signs of an attack. It usually appeared a couple of hours before the onset.

"Want to use the inhaler?"

"Uh-uh."

"I think it'll help. Make it easier for you to breathe."

"Okay, if you say so." Anthony gasped. Even that short a statement put him over the edge. It would take a couple of minutes for him to rebound to the teetering stability.

"I'll get it," Roseanne said.

Fontanelli rubbed his son's stomach, trying to get him to relax. Tension only made breathing more difficult. He still wondered whether there was an emotional component to the disease. The old wisdom said yes; the new science said no. This was a case where he sided instinctively with the old. He couldn't remember a single serious attack that didn't have some family crisis as a harbinger.

When Roseanne returned with the inhaler, he quickly assembled it, realizing ruefully that it was now old hat for him. Practice did indeed make perfect. He inserted the pressurized capsule into the inhaler and blew up the thin plastic bellows. It made a squeak, like a leaky concertina. "Too fast, huh, sport?"

Anthony nodded.

Fontanelli held it for him. Anthony took the mouthpiece and his father filled the bellows with a shot from the capsule. Anthony inhaled, held for five, then exhaled. They did it twice more, but without adding medicine. He handed the device to Roseanne, who set it on a nearby bureau. "That ought to hold you, son. If you need me, tell Mom, okay?"

Fontanelli stepped out of the room and patted Roseanne on the shoulder. "Keep an eye on him. I'll be with Belasko." He walked back down to the den where Bolan waited impatiently.

"Anything?"

"It stopped, and I wrote the number down. The menu told me to press any key to continue the search. I got all six numbers right here."

"Okay. Let's see what we got." Fontanelli dropped into the chair and punched in the first number Bolan had written down. The screen rolled, and Fontanelli fiddled with the monitor. The phone rang, and he cursed. "You'll have to take that on another phone. I got the modem on-line here. There's another phone in the kitchen."

Bolan nodded and sprinted toward the kitchen. He punched the blinking button and picked up the receiver. "Hello."

"Is that you, Striker?"

"Yeah, Hal. What's up?"

"Nothing good. Three barrels were just fished out of the Hackensack River."

"Anybody we know?"

"Two, so far. Califano and Hartford. The ME's still trying to piece them together. Literally. Somebody took them apart with a chain saw."

"Looks like we must be on to something."

"I'd say. No luck on the other two, yet. Franklin Jeffries has just disappeared. He was at the office on Saturday. His car's still in the garage. That's all we got on him. Peter Cummings doesn't answer his phone. I've contacted the Bahamian authorities. I'm waiting to hear. How's it going? Anything since the snowmobile assault team?"

"No, so far so good."

"You sure you don't want backup?"

"Uh-uh. Something smells in this whole mess, Hal. I don't know whether we can trust anybody on this one. So far there's been nothing Novick, Fontanelli and I couldn't handle. And Fontanelli insists he doesn't want anybody else around. He thinks the more people there are, the easier the Mob can get to him. He says they can buy people almost anyplace."

"It's a wonder he trusts you and Novick."

"I'm not sure he does, and I'm not sure I blame him. Listen, I'm not going to tell him about Califano and Hartford. He's edgy as it is."

"Whatever you think. Listen, Striker, if you change your mind . . ."

"I know, Hal. And thanks."

"All right. I just wanted you to know. You be careful. If you turn anything up, call me. Day or night."

"Will do."

Bolan hung up and stood there for a long moment. He wondered how much more peaceful the world must have seemed when it took weeks instead of seconds to spread bad news. It made him uncomfortable to consider the notion.

He checked his watch. It was almost time to relieve Novick on the outside. He grabbed his coat on the way back to check in with Fontanelli. Roseanne was coming down the stairs as he reached the doorway of the den. He stood aside and let her brush past him.

"Dom, he's getting worse. I don't like it."

Fontanelli sighed. "I guess I better call the doctor." He stood and walked toward the doorway. Bolan stopped him with a raised hand.

"The monitor just went."

Fontanelli whirled. Sure enough, the screen was blank. The LED on the modem was still on, but the line indicator on the phone itself was dark. "Shit!" Fontanelli shut the modem down and picked up the phone. He held the receiver to his ear. "It's dead. The bastards must have cut the line."

"Maybe not," Bolan suggested, indicating Roseanne with a flick of his eyes. "The weather might have taken a line out. It's snowing pretty hard."

"Yeah, I guess that's probably it."

"You got a CB or anything, something we could use to get a message out to get a doctor sent up here?"

"Uh-uh. I've been thinking about it, but I just never got around to it."

"Then we'll just have to take him to the doctor." Roseanne's tone was firm. It told all and sundry that anything else was out of the question. "I'll get him ready."

"Rosie, that's nuts. You can't—"

"I can and I will. If we wait too long, it will only make matters worse."

"I'll take you and the boy," Bolan said quietly.

"That isn't necessary. I can drive the Blazer."

"Yes, it *is* necessary." Bolan's tone was no less determined than her own, and she seemed to know it.

"All right. We'll be ready in ten minutes."

Roseanne raced upstairs. When she was out of sight, Fontanelli said, "She's a good woman. She means well, but she gets excited too easily, that's all. Just be firm with her and don't let her bully you."

"More easily said than done, I think," Bolan said.

Fontanelli grinned for the first time in two days. "You *are* observant."

"I'm going to tell Barry he'll have to stay out there a while longer," Bolan said. When he stepped into the cold wind, his teeth started to chatter. The snow swirled around the open door. Novick was huddled in a corner of the porch.

Bolan went to him and explained what was happening. "Mrs. Fontanelli's worried about the boy," he concluded.

"Hey, I understand. Maybe I'll have a kid someday. I'm sure I'd feel the same way."

"Listen, Barry. You and I both know Fontanelli's going to come out here and tell you he'll relieve you for a while. Whatever you do, don't let him muscle you into that. Make him stay inside with his other son."

"Roger."

"I don't know how long I'll be gone. I'll bring the communications unit with me, but I'll be out of range for most of the trip. If you run into trouble, give it a try. If I can't hear you, I'll be too far away to help, anyway."

Novick was silent for a moment. He seemed to be thinking about something particular, debating whether or not to mention it. Finally he shook his head, as if to say what the hell. He leaned toward Bolan to make sure he could be heard above the wind. "This is going to get worse before it gets better, isn't it?"

"I hope not."

"You hope not, but you think so. Am I right?"

"Yeah, you're right. You want out?"

"No way."

"If you change your mind, just say so. I can get a replacement for you if it's necessary."

"Are you kidding? You're talking to the one and only, the original, irreplaceable man."

"I appreciate your being here—"

"Listen, the kid needs a doctor. You better go."

Bolan clapped Novick on the shoulder. "I'll make it quick."

"Don't rush on my account. I kind of like the weather here. You know, as bad as it is, it's better than a five-degree day back east. Makes you feel alive, this does."

Bolan waved as he made his way back to the front door.

Roseanne was just slipping into her coat as the warrior slammed the door. Her husband had donned a parka, and he cradled Anthony carefully in his arms, making sure the boy's labored breathing wasn't hampered any further by pressure.

"Where do you think you're going?" Bolan asked.

"I'm going with you."

"No way. You have to stay here. We can't leave the lodge unattended, and Barry can't watch the outside and your son, too. I can't let you go out there. You're safer here."

Fontanelli nodded grudgingly. "All right. At least let me carry him to the Blazer."

Bolan agreed, and Fontanelli led him to the tunnel entrance, Roseanne trailing behind. With Fontanelli's direction, Bolan opened the door and climbed down into the tunnel, which was dark and cold. A slight draft blew through the underground passage. Fontanelli nudged a light switch with his elbow, flooding the tunnel with dim light.

They moved quickly through to the garage, where Fontanelli again directed Bolan through the next two doors. When Roseanne was ensconced in the rear seat, Bolan and Fontanelli handed the boy through to her. She cradled him in her lap and bent to whisper encouragement to him.

The child's raspy, constricted breath echoed eerily in the Blazer, audible even over the rumble of the engine. Fontanelli's last words before he went back underground kept reverberating in Bolan's ears. "You take good care of my boy."

Bolan hadn't answered.

What could he say?

15

Baldridge Road was indistinguishable from the snow that swept up both sides of the pass. A narrow gap, cut by the road builders, funneled the wind and collected the snow. The Blazer sat high on its frame, its blocky shape buffeted from side to side as the strong winds, compressed by the gap, ripped past it. It was like driving in a wind tunnel.

In the back seat, Anthony Fontanelli sucked at the air, his lungs bubbling, straining to get enough oxygen from each strangled gasp. Roseanne crooned to the boy. Bolan could see her in the rearview mirror, bending over the boy and smoothing his hair with nervous fingers.

Walton was twenty miles away. Under ordinary circumstances it would be a half-hour drive, perhaps a little more. But this night was far from ordinary. The thick tires of the Blazer, even with their deep treads, were no match for the slippery surface. Clotted with snow, they became slick, and the balance between control and a downhill skid was precarious.

Bolan suddenly saw headlights in the mirror. He clicked on the rear wiper, and it swept a semicircle of glass clear. The lights were moving toward him, slowly closing the gap. Instinctively he reached for the butt of the M-16 he'd recovered from the snowmobile hit team.

"You have many neighbors around here?" Bolan asked. He tried to keep his voice flat, like a man just making conversation to kill time, but Roseanne reacted immediately. She snapped her head around to look behind them.

"Oh God! They're following us, aren't they?"

"I don't know. Let's not assume the worst."

"This is all Guido's fault. That horrid old man…he did this. To his own son. How could he be so heartless?"

"Maybe he didn't have a choice, Mrs. Fontanelli."

"He had a choice. He knew Dominick didn't want anything to do with his 'friends.' He could have left Dominick alone. Left us all alone."

"It's not that easy."

"What do you know about it? For all I know you're no better than they are."

"I know more than you think."

"Sure you do."

Bolan lapsed into silence, keeping an eye on the lights that were slowly drawing closer.

The Blazer headed into a series of tricky curves. The sign warning of the impending change in the road, its standard half buried in deep snow, bore a legend that looked like a black serpent. Bolan gripped the wheel a little tighter, fighting the drag and the Blazer's desire to continue in a straight line. The road was wide, but the shoulders were obscured on either side, and nearly a foot of new snow lay on the rest of the roadway.

In the red glare of his taillights, Bolan could see the deep tracks made by his wheels, stained brown at their center where the frozen mush of snow and road salt was exposed by his passage. The headlights behind him continued to come on. He could see Roseanne constantly monitoring their tail, her head swiveling to the rear window, back to her son and once again to the rear.

"How's he doing?" Bolan asked.

"Not good. Can't you go any faster?"

"Not on this road. Not if you want to get there."

"Dammit, you're just like my husband. So logical. You're all alike, you men."

"Is there some side road we can take, somewhere close?"

"Side road? We don't have time for that. Are you crazy?"

"Roseanne, if we don't find out who's following us, we might not have time at all."

"You called me Roseanne..."

"So?"

"Then you might as well call me Rosie, like Dominick does."

It was a strange way to apologize, but Bolan accepted it without comment.

"What can I call you?" she asked.

"Mike will do."

"All right then, Mike it is. There's an old mining road about a mile ahead on the left. But I don't know if the Blazer can make it, and I'm not sure we can even find it in this awful weather."

"We'd better."

The pursuer was little more than two hundred yards behind them now and he kept on coming. The headlights grew brighter and larger even as Bolan watched in the mirror. He clicked the rearview to night vision, cutting the glare.

"You'd better get on the floor, Rosie."

"On the floor? Why?"

"If this guy isn't friendly, he might not bother to try to catch us. He doesn't have to."

Roseanne grumbled but did as he suggested. She sat on her haunches, curled around to keep Anthony in place without a seat belt. She leaned over him protectively, almost pressing on the frail form stretched out on the seat.

Bolan spotted the turnoff just in time. He swung the wheel abruptly, and the Blazer slid sideways a dozen yards before its wheels dug in. The 4X4 dipped sharply as the front wheels fell off the shoulder and chewed through a narrow gully. Then it jerked sharply upward as they bit into the slope.

"Can you drive this thing?"

"Yes, why?"

"You might have to. If our friend follows us, we could be in trouble."

Bolan downshifted, and the engine snarled as the steep slope fought against him. The four big tires did their best, but the road was little more than a logging track. It was unsurfaced, rutted and littered with rocks. The wheels occasionally slipped on raw stone, and the Blazer yawed like a runaway rocket.

"Get Anthony on the floor and climb up here, quick," Bolan barked. The lights had followed them into the mining cut. They slashed from side to side, and whipped up and down as the car struggled with the same horrendous road conditions. "I was hoping he didn't have four-wheel drive," Bolan said. "But he does."

Roseanne braced herself on the back of his seat, tumbling over the seat hips first. She landed hard, banging her knee on the passenger door. Bolan kicked the gas harder, and the Blazer spurted upward, widening the gap a little. The pursuer, probably fearing a trap, had slowed a bit, giving them an additional lead.

About fifty yards farther Bolan spotted a break in the trees. It was difficult to tell what it was, but he mentally crossed his fingers and hoped he could use it for his plan. He goosed the engine again, sending the wheels into a wild spin until they caught on some rough ground. The Blazer lurched still higher up the slope. As he reached the break, he spun the Blazer in a tight circle. It nearly capsized, and Bolan held his breath. Anthony rolled around on the floor, and Roseanne reached back to hold him steady.

"What the hell are you doing?" Roseanne hollered.

A narrow road, little more than a trail, left the mining cut at an acute angle. Bolan reached for the M-16. "Get ready," he growled. "Over here."

He scrunched toward the door, making room for Roseanne on the edge of the driver's seat. "Grab the wheel." The road juked to the left, and the light diminished. Bolan knew he'd never have a better chance. He forced his door open against the wind. Snow lashed his naked wrist and swarmed into the open cab like frozen bees. "When I jump, you just keep straight on. Don't stop, and don't look back, whatever happens. If this thing curls around and comes back this way, keep an eye out for me."

"But—"

"Just do it, Rosie. It's our only chance."

Bolan jumped, dragging the M-16 after him. He landed on his hip and rolled twice. The door banged closed, and the Blazer struggled on through the narrow slash among the trees.

Bolan scrambled through deep snow, dropping behind a drift-covered log as the onrushing 4X4 drew closer. By the outline behind the lights, he could tell it was another Blazer. He looked left and saw Roseanne's taillights disappear around a bend. Bolan swung the M-16 around, bracing it on the log. He thought about shooting out the Blazer's tires, but the crippled vehicle might be difficult to move, and there might not be an outlet for the road on the other end.

When the Blazer was twenty yards away, he fired a short burst, scattering slugs across the hood. Sparks flew like sudden fireflies, then vanished. The echo of gunfire sailed away among the trees, swallowed by the wind. The Blazer swerved to one side. The driver lost control and it slammed into a tree. Bolan charged out from behind the snow mound as the vehicle's doors flew open. The driver tumbled out into the snow and lay still.

A second man, in the passenger seat, raised his hands. Bolan raced toward the stuttering vehicle, keeping to a crouch. The driver groaned and got to his knees. Bolan moved to the rear of the 4X4, where he could see both men.

"You're in big trouble, pal," the passenger said.

"I can see that," Bolan replied. "Why were you following us?"

"It's my job."

"Is that what they call it now? A job?"

"What else? Do you know what's going on here?"

"Suppose you tell me all about it? You can start by telling me who you are."

The man reached into his coat, raising his other hand to show he wasn't going for a weapon. "Can you read, buddy?"

He flipped a small leather case. Bolan resisted the impulse to catch it, letting it land in the snow. Then, keeping the M-16 trained on the man's midsection, he bent to retrieve it. In the reflection of the headlights, he could see an official-looking identification card, encased in plastic.

"FBI?" Bolan said.

"That's right, asshole." He slapped the side of the Blazer. "And this is government property."

16

Headlights appeared suddenly, and Bolan recognized the Blazer as it bounced back into the cut. Roseanne had made a long loop. Their detour led nowhere, curling back on itself. Bolan stepped to the disabled vehicle and shot out its tires. He bent over the groaning man on the ground and snatched his wallet and a soft black leather case. Flipping it open, he found a second ID card. This one, too, purported to identify its bearer as a Special Agent of the Federal Bureau of Investigation.

"What are you going to do now?" the standing man asked. His voice cracked, betraying his nervousness.

"Nothing." Bolan backed toward Fontanelli's Blazer, keeping his eye on the man. "You'd better see to your friend."

"You're not going to leave us here?"

"Why not? I don't know whether these cards are genuine."

"How will we get back?"

"You should have thought of that." Bolan could hear the Blazer idling a few yards behind him and reached for it blindly. Feeling the hot metal of the hood, he eased his way around the front of the vehicle. Roseanne slid over to make room for him in the driver's seat. Bolan climbed in and slammed the door.

He kicked the 4X4 into gear and jerked the wheel. Jouncing down the rut, he concentrated on his driving.

"Well?" Roseanne said.

"Well what?"

"Are you going to tell me who they were?"

"They claim to be FBI."

Roseanne waited for an amplification. When it was obvious none would be forthcoming, she asked, "Were they?"

"I don't know. Maybe."

"What did they want?"

"I didn't ask."

"Oh." She snapped her lower jaw like a bear trap. Men infuriated her. Silent men made her blind with anger and frustration.

"Look," Bolan said. "I don't know who they are, not really, and there's nothing else I can tell you. What would be the point of speculating?"

"It might make me feel better."

"Sorry," Bolan said. "That's not my job. Whether you live or die, that's my concern. How you feel is something you have to deal with on your own."

"Nothing fazes you, does it?"

"Should it?"

"Never mind."

Bolan turned back onto the highway. He thought about Roseanne's silence for a moment, wondering whether it was colder inside the Blazer or outside. He drove the rest of the way without talking. The dim lights of Walton appeared through the swirling snow. "Where's the doctor?"

"Let's go to the hospital. They'll call him. He might even be there."

"On a night like this?"

"Well, he's not playing golf, we know that much, anyway."

Bolan chuckled.

"You should laugh more often," she said. "It gets easier if you do."

Bolan pulled into the hospital parking lot, leaving the Blazer nose-in toward a wall next to the emergency entrance. He jumped down from the vehicle and walked around to Roseanne's door. He helped her down, then reached in to gather Anthony in his arms. The boy was still breathing roughly, and his face was lightly flushed.

Roseanne held the door and Bolan ducked through. "Where to?" he asked over his shoulder.

"Straight ahead. The desk is around to the left at the end of the hall." They followed a blue tape line on the corridor floor, Bolan half sprinting. The boy weighed next to nothing in his arms. At the desk he stood to one side, while Roseanne explained the problem.

The nurse indicated a cubicle that was half surrounded by a sliding curtain. "Take him in there. Someone will be with you in a moment." All business, she turned then to Roseanne. "Who is your medical insurer?"

Bolan stepped into the cubicle and laid the boy on a padded table. In the background, he could hear the sharp, irritated murmur of Roseanne Fontanelli responding to the admitting nurse's questions. Anthony stirred slightly, and Bolan reached out to make sure the boy didn't fall off the table. When all the questions had been answered to the nurse's satisfaction, Roseanne joined him.

"The doctor's out on a call. They'll page him. In the meantime, they're going to give him a shot to ease his breathing."

"I'll be right back," Bolan said.

He walked back down the hall to a pay phone. He dropped a quarter into the appropriate slot then backed away from the receiver to ease the pain of the dial tone snarling in his ear. After two rings, an automated voice informed him the number he had called was out of service.

He retrieved the quarter and dropped it a second time. After punching Brognola's number, he turned to keep his back to the wall. After a half dozen rings, the operator picked up, and he gave her the requisite collect-call information. A woman came on the line. The operator relayed his request for Brognola, and he waited while she patched him through. He slipped the two ID cards out of his pocket and scrutinized them while the insipid Muzak droned away in his ear.

Brognola finally got on the line. Without preamble, Bolan said, "You know anything about FBI watching Fontanelli?"

"Good morning to you, too. What is it, one a.m. out there?" Brognola coughed once, then continued. "No, I don't. Why?"

"I'll give you some names and numbers, and you can see what you can find out." He read the information off the two cards.

"Trouble?" Brognola asked.

"Some."

"It hasn't been any too peaceful here, either. They found Franklin Jeffries late this evening. I called, but the line was down."

"What about Jeffries?"

"Strangled. The wire was still embedded in his throat. It looked familiar. Remember the DiFalco brothers? This one had Pete DiFalco written all over it. We're going to rattle his cage a little. As soon as we find him, that is."

"You think he's headed this way?"

"Yeah, Striker, I do. You be careful."

"I'll call you when I can." He hung up without saying goodbye.

Bolan went outside and leaned against the wall, keeping to the shadows under the carport. He couldn't shake the feeling that the two men who had followed them were the genuine article. What he couldn't understand was why. And why Brognola didn't know about them. Justice was a big house, and it had a lot of rooms. Few people, even the attorney general, knew what went on in all of them. But that should have worked both ways.

Brognola had certainly kept Fontanelli under his hat. But if someone in the Justice Department knew about it, he had to have gotten his information from somewhere. That could only mean that there was a leak in Brognola's group or that the information had been fed *into* the department from outside.

Bolan remembered a time several years before, when the Mob had gotten to a secretary in a regional office of the Bureau. She had managed to obtain the new identities and the whereabouts of a handful of informants who had gone into the Witness Protection Program. Despite what it liked to believe, and especially what it liked the public to believe, the Bureau was neither perfect nor invulnerable. But a secretary can't assign agents to a surveillance team. That took clout.

The next time he talked to Brognola, he'd have to tell the big Fed to track backward. If these guys *were* the genuine article, it should be possible to find out who had assigned them. You pull *his* coat, and you find out who told him to move. Back up the chain, link by link, you could maybe find something. But more than likely it would all boil down to an anonymous tip. Somebody on the inside would know where it had originated, but he wouldn't be talking about it.

Bolan moved over to the door and leaned against the glass, cupping his face to the window so he could see through it. Everything inside seemed normal. There had been little movement before, and there was little now. On a night like this, that was probably the norm. It would take a real emergency to get anyone out in this weather.

Turning away from the glass, Bolan stared out into the swirling storm. A black van sat idling across the parking lot. Its taillights threw a red glaze over the snow around it, shading into amber down along the side where the running lights glowed in the front fenders. The small antenna on the van's roof caught his eye almost accidentally.

He had seen one like it, and he knew where. Bolan opened the door casually and slipped inside as if the cold had gotten to be too much for him. He moved down the hall at a leisurely pace. Once he gained the reception area, he sprinted toward the twin glass doors of the main entrance. The same dim light bathed the canopy of the main entrance. Immediately to either side, the light was swallowed up by the night. Bolan edged into the darkness, then dropped to a crouch to sprint in among the staff cars scattered randomly in the front parking lot.

Moving to his left, he could just make out the tail-lights of the black van. Dancing from car to car, keeping low, Bolan narrowed the distance between himself and the van. In a far corner of the lot, a large delivery van bearing the words Michaelson Medical Supplies sat in the snow. It hadn't been moved for at least a day, judging by the curled breaker of snow left along its side by the plow. There was thirty feet clear between Bolan and the delivery truck, but the warrior had no alternative. If he was going to get close to the van, this was the only way.

He dashed across the open space, tumbled into the mounded snow in a shoulder roll and landed upright behind the tail of the medical truck. He pulled the silenced Beretta from its holster and crawled behind the truck on hands and knees. He watched the van for more than a minute, looking for a sign that indicated he'd been seen.

The small windows in the rear doors of the van were curtained in black, and its sides had no windows at all. If the vehicle's occupants were going to see him, it would have to be in the sideview mirrors. But there was no cover between the truck and the van. For half the forty feet between the two vehicles, they could see him in either mirror. Once he got that close, he'd be inside the blind spot.

Nothing was easy.

He considered crawling, but knew that if they spotted him, their reaction would be quick. Better to be on his feet and have a chance. He took a deep breath. Footing was treacherous on the slippery ice covering the asphalt. He nearly slipped and fell, careening sideways a couple of steps before regaining his balance. He held his breath until he was just behind the rear doors.

So far, luck was with him. Bolan pressed an ear against the cold metal of the van. He could hear voices, but the words were indistinguishable, as if the men inside were whispering. It wasn't possible to tell how many men were inside, but he knew there had to be at least two.

The doors could possibly be locked, so he'd have to coax at least one man out into the storm. Propping one foot on the rear bumper, he grabbed a chrome luggage rack and hauled himself onto the roof. His left knee banged into the roof, and he heard one of the men clearly say, "What the hell was that?"

"I dunno. You check. It's your turn."

"Hell, no. This ain't rotation, Paulie. I'm driving, you do it."

"Shit!"

Bolan slid toward the passenger side, the Beretta gripped in his right hand. He gathered his legs beneath him as the door latch clicked. The door inched open slowly, and Bolan could hear the hum and rushing air of the van's heater. A headful of tight dark curls suddenly appeared in the opening.

"See anything?" a voice, which Bolan took to be the driver's, asked.

"Hell, let me get out of the damn truck first, why don't you? Jesus!"

Then Paulie hauled himself out to stand on the snow-covered parking lot. It was now or never. Bolan launched himself, using the roof rack to brace his feet as he leaped off the van. He flipped in the air, grabbing Paulie by the coat and hauling him to the ground. Caught by surprise, Paulie seemed stunned. Bolan was up and pointing the Beretta as the smaller man struggled to get to his knees.

"Easy, go easy," Bolan cautioned. The driver shouted, and Bolan heard the far door open. He grabbed Paulie and spun him around, jamming the muzzle of the Beretta under the man's right ear. Paulie was still too stunned to struggle. Bolan hauled the man away from the van and maneuvered Paulie in front of him as the driver came around the front bumper.

"Hey, who the hell are you? Hey!" The driver seemed no less stunned than Paulie. He held an automatic pistol in his hand, and it wavered somewhere between Paulie's midsection and his head.

"Drop your gun on the ground," Bolan snapped.

"No way, man."

"You want your buddy here to get hurt?"

The driver fired twice. The first slug slammed into Paulie's chest, knocking him back into Bolan. The second slipped through Paulie's coat, grazing his ribs before slicing through Bolan's parka just above the hip. "I never liked the son of a bitch." The driver laughed, raising the gun to fire a third shot.

Before the guy could pull the trigger, Bolan shoved Paulie's deadweight forward with both hands. The body collapsed in front of the driver, who slipped as he backed away. Bolan fired once, catching the driver in the throat. The wounded man gurgled and fell backward, clutching at his collar. The gun lay on his chest for a moment, then slid off into the snow.

Bolan quickly went through both men's pockets, but he found nothing, not even a driver's license. He kicked the driver's gun away and checked Paulie, but he knew even as he knelt down there was no point.

Paulie's glazed eyes stared up at him, a few flakes of snow already melting on their unblinking lids.

Bolan searched the truck and found three Uzi machine pistols and two dozen clips. He carted the munitions to the Blazer and tossed them inside before locking it.

The parking lot was still deserted, except for the dead man and his dying companion. Bolan walked through the emergency entrance and found Roseanne still waiting in the cubicle.

"We have to go," he said.

"The doctor hasn't been here yet. We can't—"

"We don't have time. How is he?"

"The shot helped, but he needs a breathing treatment. I don't have the equipment." She nodded toward a small compressor on a wheeled table. It sprouted wires and plastic tubing, and a breathing mask dangled at one end of a corrugated blue tube. Bolan unplugged the machine and tucked it under his arm.

"What about the medicine?" he asked.

Roseanne pointed to a box of vials. "That's it."

"Can you use this thing?"

"If I have to, yes. I've seen it done enough times."

"Then let's go." He stuffed the box of vials into a pocket.

"But—"

"Roseanne, listen to me. Two men just got shot in the parking lot. One is dead and the other soon will be. They were after you and Anthony. It's not safe here."

Roseanne scooped Anthony off the table. She glared at Bolan, but he had already turned away. As they hurried toward the door, the nurse called after them, starting to round the admitting desk. Roseanne waved her off. "Tell the doctor we couldn't wait."

17

The day dawned bright and clear. The sun glinted off the thick snow and hurt the eyes. Overhead the sky was a pure blue, deeper than any Bolan had seen in a long, long time. He stepped out to the patio and scanned the compound. Huge drifts, bigger than cars, covered everything. Shrubs had been reduced to vague mounds, their leaves and branches no longer discernible beneath the gently undulating curves of the snow.

The outbuildings, half buried on the windward side, looked as if they'd been dwarfed by some mysterious process. Their roof lines were blurred by the thick covering of snow clinging to their shingles. Even the trees seemed to have shrunk. Snow was piled like sectioned cones against their trunks, and thick clots of it clung to the rough bark.

Moving away from the house, the Weatherby slung over his left shoulder, Bolan began his patrol of the grounds. As he neared the garage, he looked up at the lodge and at the towering trees beyond it, their branches thickly layered with snow. In the slight breeze, the branches stirred, discharging small puffs that scattered in the wind and triggered other puffs as they hit the branches below.

The wind was a silent presence. Bolan could feel it on his skin and see signs of its passing in the elastic movement of the trees, but it was as quiet as the surface of the moon. Climbing downhill, away from the lodge, he walked as far as the first bend in the approach road. He wore snowshoes that hissed as they glided over the soft snow. His gait was sluggish, but without the shoes, movement would have been impossible.

A day this quiet and this beautiful, he thought, was what life was supposed to be all about.

Bolan heard a shout above him and watched as little Dominick raced across the patio and jumped into the snow. The boy was ecstatic. He hurled snow into the air and raced around like an unchained puppy, his pent-up energy totally out of control. Bolan smiled and even envied the boy a little. To be that free, to be that much at liberty to go with pure instinct, was something he could understand and appreciate.

As Bolan started to climb back toward the house he heard the deep-throated rumble of an engine behind and below him, and whirled to see what caused it. Through the trees that wound toward the highway, he caught the outline of a metal box, then realized with a start that it was the turret of an armored personnel carrier. Bolan started forward, until it dawned on him the Weatherby was no match for the vehicle. Floundering toward the lodge, the snowshoes a hindrance, he struggled to get to the boy before the APC.

Like a man watching himself in slow motion on a screen, Bolan sensed that he was losing ground. His legs felt leaden as he struggled to haul them above the snow for each step. But the violence of his movement was too much for the delicate crust beneath him. Every step broke through the feathery snow, and each time he moved a foot it dragged through the resistant white fluff.

Out of the corner of his eye, he could see the APC as it broke through the trees at the bottom of the hill. He could hear the clank of its treads. Probably a half-track, he thought, as it chewed its way up the snow-cluttered approach road. He shouted for Dominick, but the boy didn't respond. Bolan pushed himself, finding a rhythm and moving more easily over the snow. He dodged among the trees like a slaloming skier, leaning left or right to skirt the thick tree trunks with as little change of direction as possible.

The half-track continued its climb, only its turret visible over the mounded snow on either side of the road. The driver seemed to be in no hurry, letting the powerful engine work at little more than a fast idle. Like the fin of a shark, the turret glided inexorably uphill, slowly closing on the parking area in front of the lodge.

The clank of the metal tracks shattered the silence, and it echoed off the mountainside in a hundred diminishing reverberations. Under it all, the steady drone of the big diesel provided an ominous undercurrent, as foreboding as a movie sound track. The APC headed into the last curve. The final hundred and fifty yards was a straightaway, true enough for a bowling alley.

Desperately Bolan watched the door of the lodge, hoping someone inside had heard the racket. But the door stayed closed. The turret started to rise above the snow, like the conning tower of a surfacing submarine. Suddenly a white star, brilliant in the bright sun, flashed at Bolan over the ridge of snow. It was the six-pointed emblem of the county sheriff. Bolan broke out of the last stand of trees as the APC drifted to a halt in the parking area.

He covered the last twenty yards as the turret hatch lifted and fell back with a clank. Calling to little Dominick, Bolan jumped over the snow ridge and dropped to the asphalt pad, the foot-deep snow cushioning his landing. The boy had finally heard him. He looked at Bolan then dashed off like a rabbit, turning the corner of the lodge and disappearing. Before Bolan could run after him, a Stetson bobbed up and out of the turret. The beefy red face it shaded looked around suspiciously. Seeing Bolan, the man said, "You Fontanelli?"

"He's inside," Bolan replied. He started to go after Dominick, when he saw Novick charge up the hill in hot pursuit.

The man hauled himself up and out of the turret, landing on the deck of the APC with a crack of high-heeled boots. The man watched Bolan closely, staring back over his shoulder even while he climbed down to the ground.

The man must have stood six feet four or five. He wore brown uniform pants over his boots, and a split-leather suede jacket with a thick sheepskin lining. On his hip, in an elaborately stitched holster strapped to his thigh with a rawhide thong, rode a pearl-handled Colt. He stepped to one side as two more men climbed up and out, dressed identically.

The big man slapped the side of the APC. "Handy sucker in these parts. We get some nasty snows up here, but they don't bother this baby. Thank God for Army surplus." He laughed, but there was no joy in the sound.

"Name's Greenway, Walt Greenway. Sheriff around here." Greenway watched Bolan to see whether his announcement had made an impression. When Bolan said nothing, he continued. "Let's go find ourselves Mr. Dominick Fontanelli."

Without waiting for an answer, he brushed past Bolan. As he strode toward the patio steps, he called back over his shoulder, "Who might you be?"

Bolan hesitated for a beat. Greenway noticed and cocked an ear. "I didn't catch that."

"Belasko, Mike Belasko."

Greenway grunted. "You work for Fontanelli, do you?"

"Just a friend."

"What do you do for a living, if you don't mind my asking."

"I do mind."

"Uh-huh." Greenway bounded up the steps more easily than Bolan would have guessed for a man that size. The warrior glanced around, looking for little Dominick. He opened the door and stepped aside for Greenway to enter. The sheriff whistled as he scrutinized the interior of the lodge. "Nice place. Fontanelli must be rolling in it, huh?"

"You'll have to ask him."

"Ask me what?" Dominick Fontanelli stood at the top of the stairs.

"Never mind," Greenway said. "You Fontanelli?"

"I'm Dominick Fontanelli, yes."

"Walt Greenway, Walton County sheriff." Again he failed to extend his hand.

"What can I do for you, Sheriff?"

"Your boy was in to the hospital last night, that right?"

"That's right."

"Mind if I ask why?"

"Not at all. He was having an asthma attack. My wife took him in for treatment."

"You go with her, did you?"

"No, as a matter of fact I didn't. Why?"

"'Cause the nurse says there was a big fellow with her. A fellow about your size, I'd say."

"No, I wasn't there."

"I was with her," Bolan said.

"Were you now? You folks didn't hang around long enough to see the doc, though, did you? You and Mrs. Fontanelli . . . ?"

Fontanelli looked at Bolan before answering. "No, that's right. They gave him a shot and it seemed to help. Roseanne thought it might be better to bring him home and look after him here."

"Can I talk to the little woman?"

"What?" Fontanelli seemed confused.

"Your wife. Can I talk to her?"

"I don't see why not. She's upstairs with Anthony. I'll go get her."

"I'd appreciate it." Greenway watched him walk back up the stairs, then turned to Bolan again.

"You're pretty handy with a gun, are you, Belasko?"

"Why?"

"Because I got four dead bodies on my hands. Something tells me you know more than a little bit about that."

"Four dead men?" Bolan was startled.

"Yes, sir, four. Two at the hospital and two more up an old timber road between here and there."

18

Greenway left after asking Roseanne a few cursory questions. "What's going on here?" she asked.

"What do you mean?" Dominick questioned.

"I'm talking to him," she snapped, stabbing a finger at Bolan. "Answer me. You said there were two men. Why was he talking about four?"

Bolan shook his head, wondering the same thing. He didn't want to tell Roseanne, but it was obvious that the two men who had followed them off the road had been killed, most probably by the two men in the black van. Someone had apparently been following the followers. Bolan no longer wondered whether the claim of being FBI was bogus. He knew it wasn't.

Someone had pulled strings and let the FBI do the stalking. It had been a simple matter to sit back and wait while they did the legwork. All that remained was to move in and take Fontanelli down. If that meant a couple of unsuspecting agents got wasted in the process, well, those were the breaks.

"Where's Junior?" Roseanne asked.

"He was outside, playing," Bolan replied. "I saw Barry out there with him."

"I don't want him outside playing. I want him in here, where he's safe."

"Then go get him," her husband barked. "Jesus, Rosie!"

Roseanne stormed over to the door and jerked it open. She stepped onto the patio, tugging her sweater around her to ward off the biting cold. "Junior!" she called. Her voice cut through the interior silence like a serrated knife. "Junior!" She was making a point and wanted both men to know it.

Fontanelli shrugged into his parka and walked out after her. "Go on inside, Rosie. I'll get him." He shoved her gently toward the doorway. She made a brief show of resisting, then walked inside, glaring at Bolan on her way to the stairs.

Bolan grabbed the Weatherby and followed Fontanelli outside. He was uneasy, and thought he might have made a mistake leaving the boy in Novick's charge. The lieutenant was a good cop, but this was the major league. A sandlot star cut very little ice with the big boys. You either had it or you didn't. The jury was still out on Barry Novick.

Fontanelli called out, "Dominick, come on inside. Dominick?"

When he got no answer, he stepped down onto the snow and took a few steps. "Dominick?"

Still no answer. Bolan felt a chill that had nothing to do with the temperature. He leaped down behind Fontanelli. "Go inside. I'll take care of it."

"No way. He's my kid. I'll find him."

Bolan recognized the guilt that lay behind the man's determination. Like most high-level executives, Dominick Fontanelli had had too little time to spare for his family. And he blamed himself, as if he had made a choice at their expense.

"Where the hell is he?" Fontanelli exploded. "Where's Novick?"

He trudged toward the rear of the lodge, calling at regular intervals, as if he were some machine programmed to repeat incessantly until getting a response. Each time, his voice trailed off over the frozen mountainside, dwindling away to a faint, unintelligible trill. Fontanelli started to run, then stopped suddenly, realizing he didn't know where to go.

Bolan sprinted after him, nearly colliding with him at the abrupt halt. "Let's take this systematically, Dominick. We'll start up there. That's where I saw them last." Bolan pointed up the mountainside toward a stand of tall trees. A broken line of footprints betrayed the passage of at least one set of feet, but the holes in the snow were too large to have been Junior's.

Fontanelli started to follow them, but floundered badly in the waist-deep drifts. He seemed suddenly to understand that passion wouldn't serve him well. "Wait here," he said. "I'll get some snowshoes."

Bolan nodded.

He turned to watch the distraught man wander back toward the lodge. When Fontanelli disappeared inside, the warrior turned to look up the hillside. The tracks in the snow wound uncertainly toward a stand of pines. Other than the ruptured surface, there wasn't a single sign of human presence. The sun was high overhead, its piercing light glinting off the surface undiminished. Bolan squinted against the glare, but saw no more than he had with his eyes wide open. He fished in his pocket for a pair of sunglasses.

Bolan started up the mountain, kicking his way along the broken snow path. He'd gone no more than

twenty yards when he heard Fontanelli call him from
the patio. "Wait for me."

When Dominick caught up to him, both men belted
on snowshoes and started toward the trees, this time
keeping to the left of the trail, where the snowshoes
had a flat surface to press against. Even in the cold air
it was hot work. Sweat glistened on their foreheads
and trickled down their necks. The higher they
climbed, the more Bolan realized it was unlikely little
Dominick would have made the climb by himself. That
was troubling enough. But Novick's disappearance
was cause for even greater concern.

Bolan stopped once to shout Novick's name, but his
voice just slapped back at him, the sharpness of the
consonants cracking like a bullwhip once or twice before vanishing into thin air.

As they drew near the trees, Bolan hoped to find
both of them, man and boy, crouched behind a snowdrift, a foolish grin pasted on reddened faces. But he
knew that was unlikely. Novick would know, even if
Junior didn't, that their situation was too delicate for
such a joke.

They reached the trees, out of breath. And as Bolan had feared, the footprints continued on through
the stand and up the mountain beyond.

"He would never come up here alone," Fontanelli
gasped. "Something's terribly wrong."

But Bolan said nothing. He'd seen—and hoped
Fontanelli hadn't—something more ominous than the
mocking silence that greeted every shout. Scattered
recklessly among the broken clods of snow like the
crumbs from Hansel's hand, bright red flecks had
sunk into the white fluff, carried an inch or two below the surface by their own heat.

The blood was fresh.

Bolan also noticed a change in the character of the footprints. They seemed more chaotic, as if the man who made them was out of control or, just as likely, as if there were actually two sets, and the second set had begun to diverge from the first. The man who'd made the second set had either tired or had lost strength more rapidly than the first.

Another stand of pines, this one sprouting up behind a cluster of snow-covered rocks, lay another hundred and fifty yards above them. "Up there." Fontanelli pointed to the trees. "He must be up there."

Bolan was troubled now by something else. Fontanelli hadn't mentioned the blood, but he must have noticed it. The drops had grown larger, the latest leaving dime-size shafts in the snow. The color was bright against the pure white background. Fontanelli's military career would have taught him to notice such things more readily than the average man. He must have noticed them, Bolan thought. Why hadn't he said anything? Before he'd even finished asking the question, Bolan realized the answer. Fontanelli couldn't mention them, because to do so was to recognize the terrible possibility they represented.

As they drew closer, Bolan noticed something beyond the distant trees. Dark and bulky against the snow, the object couldn't be a rock because it would have been covered with snow, as would anything else out in the storm. So it had to have been a recent addition to the mountain tableau. And it was motionless, too still for an animal.

Fontanelli spotted the object just after Bolan, and started to run. A terrible sound spiraled out behind him, shrill and heartrending in the cold air, ripping open the Sierra silence like the cry of an angry eagle. Bolan raced after him as best he could.

Fontanelli beat him by a step, throwing himself onto the snow and gasping for air beside the crumpled figure. Bolan took the distraught man by the shoulders and tugged him away, handling him with no more difficulty than if he were a bundle of dry sticks. He knelt beside the body, his heart pounding in his chest as he eyed the ugly red stain on the back of the dark blue coat. A bright red pool of blood, sluggish in the cold snow, glittered where windblown snowflakes had caught on its damp surface, twinkling like stars in a ruby sky.

Leaning over the still form, Bolan pressed an ear to the motionless chest. From far away, he felt rather than heard the timid thump of a heartbeat, then another and a third. It was weak, but still there. Lying on one flattened cheek, the head was cocked to the side. Bolan leaned close, hoping to hear the hiss of air. The breathing was shallow, but he almost smiled when a whispered exhalation tickled his ear.

Grasping the surprisingly heavy body by the shoulders, he rolled it onto its back. A thin trickle of blood ran down from one corner of the white-lipped mouth. The cheek that had lain against the snow was white, probably frostbitten. Bolan snatched a fistful of dry snow and rubbed it against the cheek, trying to restore a little circulation.

The eyes flickered, then opened. They wore a stunned look, a glaze glittering on their surfaces. Then the lids fluttered again, and the lips curled into a faint smile. Only then did Bolan become aware of Fontanelli sobbing behind him.

"He's coming around," Bolan said. He sensed Fontanelli's movement, then felt the bulk of the big man as he knelt in the snow to his right.

Leaning forward, Fontanelli reached out with both hands, like a supplicant in the temple.

"What happened?" he shouted. "Where's my son?"

19

Barry Novick shook his head once, then closed his eyes. Bolan opened the detective's coat and pulled up his blood-soaked shirt. The wound wasn't as bad as it had looked. The man had lost blood, but the bullet had passed through the flesh under the left arm. It didn't appear to have broken any bone. Chasing up the hill had pumped blood and weakened him.

"Can you get him down to the house?" Bolan asked, already on his feet.

"Yes. Where are you going?"

Bolan pointed to the wandering break in the snow, coiling as if a great serpent had wriggled up the mountain.

"I'm going with you," Fontanelli said.

"We can't both go. They have your son, but they haven't hurt him. And they won't, as long as they need him to get to you. If they take you, they don't need the boy. I don't have to tell you what that means, do I?"

Fontanelli shook his head. He looked up at Bolan, but the big man was already moving away on the track that wound up toward the top of the mountain. The ridge line was clean and smooth where the brilliant white of the snow abruptly shaded into the sky's deep blue.

Bolan turned once to watch Fontanelli. With Novick draped over his shoulder, Dominick was struggling toward the lodge, one painful step at a time. The Executioner turned his full attention back to the ridge. He knew he was right, that the boy was a chit, a piece in a complicated chess game, but one that would unhesitatingly be offered in exchange for the one piece in the game that really mattered—Dominick himself.

Bolan unslung the Weatherby. Carrying the big rifle lightly in one hand, he slogged toward the top of the ridge.

As he neared the crest, Bolan slowed a bit. A man standing tall was an incredibly easy target against the blue sky. On the far side, the crowns of a few trees down slope poked up like a fistful of dark green-and-white fingers. Bolan dropped to his stomach and wriggled up the last twenty yards. Taking no chances, he scooped snow away with sweeping arms, half tunneling his way to the top. When he was within a few feet of the ridge, he dug deeper, gouging a rut deep enough and broad enough to conceal him completely.

The snow was dry and feathery. It kept cascading into the tunnel, and hampered his progress. After several minutes he was finally close. The wall of snow in front of him began to glow as the sunlight filtered partway through. A few more scoops and he had a thin, translucent barrier. The frail wall glowed reddish yellow with refracted light.

Slowly, carefully, Bolan reached out with one gloved hand and scraped away at the bottom of the fiery membrane. It was too much to ask that he be able to cut a small hole all the way through without the rest crumbling. The membrane collapsed of its own

weight, and he found himself staring out at a bleakly
brilliant mountainside as uninhabited as a hermit's
dream of paradise. It was desolate, and it was ach-
ingly beautiful. Less heavily forested than the lodge
side, the mountain swept away in an almost unbroken
plane. What irregularities there were had been diminished by the accumulated snow.

And scrawled across it, like an obscene joke sprayed
on a church wall, the trail of the kidnapper wound its
way into the tree line far below.

Bolan used the Weatherby's scope to get a closer
look. He panned from left to right, stopping at every
tree for a moment, searching for any sign of movement. There was none.

At the center, where the trail wound into the trees,
he was more patient. Lingering on one tree after another, he scanned up from the snow line to a point six
feet above it, then back down before moving on to the
next. It was tempting to charge headlong over the ridge
and down, but as tempting as it was, it was also stupid.

The kidnappers knew they'd been followed. Novick
was evidence of that. For all they knew, Novick wasn't
alone. And simple prudence required that assumption. Moving on toward the right, Bolan's patience
was rewarded. A single flash of light speared out and
vanished. It had come and gone so quickly, the warrior wasn't even certain he'd seen it.

Swinging the scope back and holding it, he waited.
His arms began to ache from the strain of holding the
scope steady. Breathing deeply but slowly, Bolan tried
to keep the motion of his own body to an absolute
minimum. After three agonizing minutes, a second
flash, this one more certain, but even shorter in dur-

ation than the first, speared away from the tree. It looked almost as if the tree were sparking, discharging electricity in short, sharp bursts.

Bolan remained motionless, holding his breath. He centered the cross hairs of the scope on the tree, trying to stay loose enough to swing the big gun to either side the moment a target presented itself. A puff of smoke appeared, and Bolan exhaled. The upper hand had just shifted. The concealed gunman was either stupid or relaxed enough to grow careless. Either way, Bolan would turn it to his advantage.

"Patience," Bolan whispered.

An elbow appeared, then disappeared. Another puff of smoke wafted out from behind the tree, about three feet off the ground. The gunman apparently knelt. The arm movement was repeated three more times, but at unpredictable intervals. The exposure was so brief and so minimal that a clean shot was almost impossible, even for Bolan.

He needed something more. He needed a break, or he had to make his own. Exposing himself was out of the question, but he had to do something to draw the man out. He searched his pockets, looking for something he could use. In desperation he stripped a cigarette pack and removed the foil lining. Unplugging the earphone from the transceiver, he wrapped the phone in the bright paper then tied it with the wire.

Sighting through the scope, he backed down the slope a bit, until the rifle muzzle lay just above the snow. Raising his arm high overhead, he twirled it like an aborigine with a *chiringa*, the foil flying out and glinting in the sun. He did it once, quickly yanking the lure back out of sight.

But the man remained hidden. If he had seen the flash of sunlight on the silver, he wasn't biting. Again Bolan twirled the lure overhead, again jerking it back after a single orbit. Still nothing moved in the scope.

Bolan cursed softly, then tried a third time, twirling the paper three times before withdrawing it.

This time he scored.

A head appeared briefly around the edge of the tree. In the scope, Bolan could see a blur of moon-shaped face, the features unresolved in the quick movement. He centered the cross hairs on the edge of the trunk and waited. He considered trying it again, but rejected the thought. He didn't want to be too overt. The guy might not be stupid, just careless, lulled by inaction into a casual security. Anything suspicious might sharpen his senses. That adrenaline hit had a way of stimulating everything, especially dormant instincts.

Slowly the round face began to reemerge, like a fleshy moon rising sideways. "Wait," Bolan muttered. The full face was exposed now. Rendered in sharp detail, its features betrayed a mixture of curiosity and suspicion. The man had definitely seen something. He wanted to know what, but wasn't sure it was benign.

Bolan eased his finger snugly against the cold metal trigger. He wanted a better shot, but knew this might be his only one. At the first sign of movement, he was going to fire. Then, as if in answer to a prayer, a shoulder appeared below the round face. A hand snaked out around the tree. Thick, fleshy fingers lay against the bark as the man braced himself, getting to his feet. The shift in weight pulled the shoulder farther into the open.

Bolan squeezed. The Weatherby's thunder rolled up toward the heavens. Through the scope, the warrior saw the brief look of surprise as the heavy slug found its mark. The cheeks puffed with the impact; air expelled from the lungs made a better, rounder moon of the face. Then it vanished in a tangle of flailing arms. The man sprawled on his back in the snow.

It was now or never.

Bolan scrambled to his feet and charged over the ridge. His snowshoes hampered him, but he would never make it without them. Running parallel to the broken snow, he careered down the slope toward the fallen man. As he reached the trees, he glanced quickly toward the body. It lay on its back, dead eyes staring up at the crown of the tree.

The path wound down through the trees, and Bolan raced on. There were two tracks now, one much smaller than the other, as if the boy had walked, or been dragged, by someone too tired to carry him any longer. A single blue mitten lay half buried in the snow.

The trees thinned, and Bolan picked up his pace. The slope flattened a bit, and he felt more in control of his headlong descent. As he ran, he wondered what he expected to find. The pursuit had taken far too long for the kidnappers still to be catchable on foot. But there was a chance, however slim, that he might find something meaningful.

The snow rose abruptly, and Bolan almost pitched over the edge into a broad, shallow gully. The trail curled away to the left and he followed it. He sprinted along the gully until he found a gentle scoop in the lip of it. The tracks descended to the gully floor, and Bolan plunged after them.

Fifty yards farther on, the gully flattened out, then dropped to an old timber road. Bolan followed the tracks into the timber cut another hundred yards. He stopped, gasping for air on the edge of a large depression in the snow. it had been flattened, crushed really, but not by human feet alone.

To one side, a circle of blackened snow nearly a foot across had melted clear through to the stony earth beneath it. Protected from the slight breeze by the trees on either side, the sharp tang of exhaust still hung in the air.

Bolan crossed the disturbed area and knelt down. Leaning forward, he recognized at once what he was looking at. He reached out with his fingers to be sure, running them around the sharp edges of the first rectangular cut. He looked at the twin lines that headed down the mountain, and he cursed.

His fingers had traced the outline of a metal track.

20

"This is all your fault. Damn you!" Roseanne Fontanelli smashed her fist onto the table. A vase of dried flowers teetered precariously on its base, and Dominick reached out to steady it. Roseanne slapped his hand away, and the vase fell on its side, rolled to the edge of the table and fell off. It shattered on the floor. No one spoke while the shards rattled slowly to a halt.

In the utter silence that followed, it seemed no one wanted to be the first to speak. Finally, when she could stand it no longer, Roseanne covered her ears and shouted, "God, how I hate your father and everything he represents." She tailed off into an incomprehensible shriek. Fontanelli moved around the table, reaching for her with both hands, but she backed away. "Don't you come near me. You...just... don't..."

"Rosie, for God's sake..."

The doorbell rang, its chime tolling gently, somehow soothing in the supercharged room.

"I'll get it," Bolan said. He drew his Beretta 93-R and walked to the door. Standing to one side of the thick oak, he leaned forward to peer through one of the narrow lead glass panels. A man stood on the patio, a black bag in one hand, a slip of paper in the other. The words "Pen-Team Able" wavered behind the pebbled pane, block printed in one-inch letters. It was the signal he had arranged with Brognola.

Bolan slipped the gun back into his holster and slid the top bolt, then the bottom one. Finally, releasing the chain lock and turning the dead bolt, he pulled the door open. "Come in, Doctor. Glad you could make it so soon."

The doctor stepped inside and shrugged out of his black overcoat. As he unwound a thick scarf, he surveyed the room with a practiced eye. Tall and slender, the man appeared to be about fifty. His white hair was closely cropped, almost military in its severity. His blue eyes, so pale they were almost colorless, moved incessantly as he took stock of the situation.

"Marshall Hamilton," he said, extending his hand. The slender fingers were muscular and the grip firm. "All right," he continued, bending to retrieve his bag. "Where's the patient?" His voice was surprisingly strong, and deeper than one would have expected. "A gunshot wound, I understand?"

"Yes, and while you're here I'd like you to take a look at an asthma patient, as well."

"Lead the way."

Bolan left the Fontanellis to themselves and climbed the stairs. Hamilton was right behind him. As they walked down the carpeted hallway, Bolan could hear the argument continue below.

Novick was in a room at the end of the hall. Bolan poked his head through the dimly lighted doorway and fumbled for the light switch on the wall. Before he found it, he heard Novick shift his position in bed.

"Don't knock or anything like that," Novick called. "Just barge on in." He laughed, but his voice was weak, and the laugh died quickly.

Bolan clicked on the light. "There's a doctor in the house."

"Doctor of what?" Novick demanded. "Remember Jerry Graham, the wrestler? He was a doctor, too. Only nobody knew what of..."

"Hypnology," Hamilton said.

"What's that?"

"Not me. Graham. At least that's what he said."

"You like wrestling?" Novick was intrigued. "Maybe you're all right after all."

"If not, I have malpractice insurance." He turned to Bolan. "Where's the boy?"

"Two bedrooms down, on the left."

"I'll call you when I'm ready to look in on him. I think I can handle this one. Tough guys are easy to fix. You just give them a fistful of placebos and a shot in the butt and they heal themselves. I don't think your friend here is any different."

Bolan nodded and turned to leave as Novick sat up. As he passed through the doorway, he heard Novick ask, "You remember the Sheik? That strut of his, the Camel Walk...?"

As he neared the top of the stairs, Bolan slowed a bit. Fontanelli and his wife were still talking, but in more moderate tones. The argument seemed to be over, at least for the moment. Bolan sat on the top step, not willing to abort their reconciliation. And he needed time to think.

He'd told Brognola about Novick, but said nothing about the missing boy. Hal could only go one of two ways. If he went by the book, it would mean the FBI. If he didn't, the ball would be in Bolan's court anyway. Until they heard from the kidnappers, he didn't want to do anything that might upset the apple cart.

It seemed clear they couldn't count on help from the local law. The prints in the snow suggested unequivocally that the sheriff's half-track had been part of the kidnapping. As expected, the two FBI IDs were valid. The men themselves had been reported missing. That meant the Bureau was, at best, leaky. There was still the State Police, but Bolan wasn't keen on that one. Rather than introduce another unknown into the equation, he'd prefer to handle it himself. He was co-designer of the dilemma. He'd be damned if he'd let it fall out this way.

The first thing that had to be done was to find out exactly what the kidnappers wanted in exchange for the boy. The only way to do that was sit on his hands and wait for them to come to him. As long as they had something to trade, Fontanelli wouldn't talk. If something happened to his son, however, he'd be inclined to seek revenge. Short of killing them with his bare hands, the best thing he could do would be cooperate with an investigation.

Fontanelli's own search through the financial labyrinth of Fontanelli Industries was surrendering its gold reluctantly. So far, little more than flakes had turned up in the pan. They'd yet to find the first nugget.

But the kidnappers didn't know that. And the desperate act of snatching the boy only confirmed that the mother lode was there, somewhere. That, and their belief that Dominick Fontanelli could find it, if he looked long enough and hard enough. That it had to do with money was made more than evident by the murders of Franklin Jeffries, Anthony Califano and David Hartford.

Bolan stretched his arms above his head, suppressing a yawn. The tension was taking its toll. He groaned loudly to signal his descent, and headed downstairs. When he entered the living room, Dominick and Roseanne were seated on the sofa, talking quietly. Roseanne's face was red, and streaks of mascara stained her cheeks, but she seemed to have regained her composure somewhat.

Bolan sat opposite them.

"What do we do now?" Roseanne asked.

"We wait."

"They won't . . . hurt . . ."

"No, I don't think so. If that's all they wanted, they wouldn't have bothered to take him. If they want anything, it's Dominick. Junior can't hurt them, and they know that if they hurt *him*, they'll never get what they want from his father."

"Can't we do anything? Shouldn't Dominick call Mr. Fontanelli? Can't his father do something?"

"No," Dominick snapped. "Don't you understand? If I go to him, I'm playing by their rules. That's what they want. That's what this is all about, their rules. But nobody makes rules for me, nobody. Not anymore!"

Roseanne tilted her head to look at her husband. Her face seemed to dissolve as something slowly crystallized in her brain then found its way to her features. "He knows . . . he knows all about it already. That's what you think, isn't it? That's why you won't go to him. You think he knows. Maybe that he even engineered it. My God! What kind of a monster is he?"

Fontanelli didn't deny it. He looked at Bolan, a hopeless expression on his face.

Dr. Hamilton suddenly appeared at the foot of the stairs. "I'm ready for the boy. Perhaps his mother would like to stay with me?"

"Yes, of course," Roseanne said. She got to her feet as if she were only too glad to get away from Dominick.

The doctor looked at Bolan with a quizzical expression. When Bolan remained silent, he said, "Your friend is going to be fine. He'll be sore for a few days, but it was uglier than it was dangerous. He's lost some blood, so he'll need to rest. And make sure he gets plenty of fluids. I've given him some antibiotics intravenously, and left a supply of tablets. Give him one or, in his case, *make* him take one, every six hours until they're all gone. My compliments to the nurse. Whoever patched him up knew what he was doing. A first-class job." Then, nodding at Roseanne, he turned and went back up the stairs.

The telephone's strident bell hammered at the walls of the lodge.

Dominick dashed for the receiver, but Bolan beat him to it. He picked it up and said, "Just a minute." Cradling the mouthpiece against his leg, he whispered, "Stay calm. Don't argue with him, but don't agree to anything too quickly. We want them to stay nervous."

When he nodded Bolan handed him the phone.

MACK BOLAN WORKED patiently on the Weatherby Mark V. The sharp tang of gun oil filled the room, overwhelming the smell of wood burning in the fireplace. He pulled the cleaning rod through for the next to last time, then balled the oil-soaked cotton and tossed it into the fire. Working now with a patch of linen, he ran it through once then held the barrel to the light. The sharp edges of the rifling grooves glittered as the barrel wavered in his hand.

Dominick Fontanelli sat across the table from him, his hands clasped loosely, like those of a man who isn't sure he wants to pray, but has run out of options.

Getting to his feet, he expelled the air from his lungs in a long, whistling explosion. Bolan glanced at him, but said nothing. He knew there was nothing to be said. The time for talking had expired.

The string had been played out. This was overtime. And sudden death.

Bolan began reassembling the Weatherby. His movements were smooth, practiced without being mechanical. As many times as he had broken the gun down and put it back together, he never took a single step for granted. He worked with that unforced concentration that only the true specialist can master. The game was now in the hands of the first stringers. It was crunch time and, as always, Bolan had come to play.

When the Weatherby was assembled, Bolan wiped his hands on a clean towel. Then he slipped the bullets into the magazine with a deliberate snap. He reached behind for his coat and stuffed the box of ammo into a pocket. The warrior got to his feet and strapped on the holster for the .44.

Fontanelli watched him now. His eyes had a faraway look, like deep, still water on a cloudy day. He already wore a weapon on his hip. Over the lip of the table, Bolan could just make out the butt of the Colt Python .357 Magnum. Without a word, Fontanelli stood and slipped on his coat. He zipped it to his throat, then pulled up the bottom zipper about a foot, enough to give him access to the Python, but not enough to make him cold. He tugged on skintight leather gloves, then jerked a gray knit watch cap down over his ears.

He nodded to Bolan, then picked up the AR-15 lying across the chair next to him.

Bolan donned his jacket and adjusted the snug fit to make sure it didn't hamper his movements. When he was ready, he slung the Mark V over his shoulder, pulled gloves on and unrolled the watch cap he already wore like a beanie.

Novick shifted uncomfortably in his chair. "You're sure you don't want me to come along?"

Bolan shook his head. "Not this time, Barry. Somebody has to stay here with Roseanne and Anthony. We'll both have com packs. Call if you need us."

"Gotcha."

Fontanelli jammed several clips for the AR-15 into his pockets. He nodded to Novick and headed toward the basement door. "Make sure you lock this behind us," he said, jerking the door open. He pulled the key from the lock and tossed it to the detective, who snatched it out of the air with his good arm.

Bolan stepped through the door first and started down the stone stairs. At the bottom, he turned and waited for Fontanelli. Novick appeared in the doorway, then the door closed. It thudded home with a dull boom, and the snick of the lock was sharp and final in the cold air of the tunnel. Bolan adjusted the earphone and raised Novick on the com set. Fontanelli took over, and when they were satisfied communications were in working order, Bolan turned to start down the tunnel. Fontanelli fell in behind him, even though the tunnel was wide enough to accommodate them two abreast.

It was, Bolan realized, the man's way of telling him who was in charge. Their steps sounded hollow, the leather of their boots slapping the stone floor with a flat, dry sound, like old hands clapping fitfully. At the second door, Fontanelli turned the key and held the door while Bolan stepped through. Then he took the key and dropped it into his pocket. They moved on to the last door, each listening to the echo of their feet on the stone.

When Fontanelli moved to open the door, Bolan stopped him with a raised hand. "Remember," he said, "They have at least one laser sight. We don't know for sure they're even out there, but we can't afford to make a mistake. We'll make a quick circuit of the lodge. If we don't find anybody, we'll come back and take the Blazer. If we do... well..."

"I know."

"No heroics. You won't help your son by getting yourself killed."

Bolan let his hand drop, and Fontanelli turned the key. When the door had closed behind them, they climbed the steps to the heavy trapdoor. Bolan shoved it back, letting it fall against the chain that kept it from opening all the way. Fontanelli scrambled up after him, and Bolan lowered the door back into place.

They moved in single file out into the garage. Bolan walked to the side door and rubbed the dusty glass with his glove. Leaning over to peer up the mountainside, he could see a quarter moon, its color the stark white of fresh bone, riding above the snow line. The deep blue sky beyond sparkled with dozens of stars, visible even through the dirty windowpane.

The moonlight would be an added hazard, but it cut both ways. They could be seen, but they could also see. The snow, tinted with a pale blue wash on the drift edges and wherever shadow pooled at the base of a tree, looked more sinister than it did in daylight.

They put on snowshoes, belting them tightly to make certain they'd stay on.

"Okay," Bolan whispered. "It's time."

He pushed the door open and sprinted with a stiff-legged stride to the corner of the nearer guest cottage. Dropping to one knee, he counted to ten, then waved Fontanelli out. Using binoculars, he scrutinized the immediate periphery of the lodge. The building sat silent and dark, like a memorial to some vanished culture. Its dark wood, sharp angles etched starkly against the surrounding snow, looked ancient and immutable.

Bolan examined every shadow, every dark corner where the building changed direction. Nothing moved. The wind moaned through the trees farther up the mountain. Surface snow, ripped loose by the gusting, swirling currents, hissed across the frozen crust, collecting in loose drifts at every obstacle.

He turned the glasses on the nearest trees. Each trunk looked black as pitch, even in the moonlight. They could have been tombstones made of charcoal, their matte finishes unevenly shaded like the casual strokes of a beginning artist. The trees, too, were devoid of life. If someone lay in wait for them, he was farther away, expecting them as surely as they were looking for him. It had come, as it always did, to the perfect hunt, that symmetry of hunter and prey, each participant playing both roles, never sure which was properly his.

Bolan leaned forward to peer around the corner of the cottage. The wind slashed at him, making his cheeks sting with its icy freight. Getting to his feet, he seemed to ooze around the corner as if he were boneless, more fluid than flesh should be. Fontanelli followed him, less flexible, feeling awkward, and just a little silly. There was an undeniable foolishness about it all, he thought, grown men playing cowboys and Indians. But it was no game, and the stakes couldn't be higher.

21

The search was frustrating. In the ghostly light of the moon, which was beginning to slide behind the mountain, everything appeared to lose substance. Shadows moved, seeming more solid than they were, but everything else became transformed. The trees wavering in the wind, the swirls of snow twisting like dervishes and disappearing, even the occasional slide of snow, took on a kind of presence. It was as if everything in the landscape was alive. Bolan's eyes darted left and right, drawn to every movement, no matter how insignificant. He looked because he couldn't afford not to.

They had widened their circle now, making a second trip around the lodge, this time trying to think like the men they knew had to be there among the blue shadows. Bolan was now convinced that the kidnappers never meant to exchange the boy for his father. They merely intended to use him to draw his father outside the protection of the lodge.

But where were they and what were they waiting for?

Fontanelli was losing his edge. He trudged through the snow like a zombie. It seemed to Bolan that the man was asking to be put out of his misery, making a target of himself in the naive hope that it would all end with his death, that his son would be returned, that his family would be left alone.

The Executioner knew better.

He hoped that something would happen soon, something to galvanize Fontanelli, shoot a surge of electricity through him, to shake him out of the self-pity and the lethargy that seemed to enfold him like a burial shroud. He needed Fontanelli, and the man knew it. Bolan could see the uncertainty in the guy's face. He was torturing himself with questions, with doubts. He'd made a colossal mistake, but what he didn't seem to understand was that sacrificing himself wouldn't atone for that mistake.

The world he'd been sucked into against his will didn't understand forgiveness. It was a world so warped that justice not only wore a blindfold, she was bound and gagged as well. Innocence didn't count for anything. It was a consequence of the age.

They were behind the lodge now, two hundred yards up the slope. With the moon almost gone they'd soon be all but blind. And out there somewhere, Bolan was convinced, lay a man with a laser sight and probably night glasses, a man who would be able to see them easily, floating across his field of vision like warm red clouds. The cold and the snow not only offered them no cover, they made concealment all but impossible.

Bolan fell to the snow behind the trunk of a lodge-pole, one they'd cut down two days earlier. He stared at the lodge, trying to think along the same lines as the men he sought.

And then it struck him. It was so simple, he didn't know how he could have missed it. The point had been to smoke Fontanelli out of hiding, strip him of security. Out in the open, even with a bodyguard, they could hunt him down at will—but they had to *know* Fontanelli was outside before they could come after him. In taking the tunnel and slipping out through the garage, the two men had failed to trip the alarm. For all the hunters knew, their prey was still securely entrenched inside the lodge. If they were content to wait, they could well be there all night. If not, they'd have to make a move soon.

Bolan wriggled to the left, just far enough to train a pair of binoculars on the shadows massed around the lodge. It made sense, now. Why position yourself hundreds of yards away from your target when you could sit much closer and wait for him to come to you? And the answer was just as simple. There *was* no reason.

Only two doors remained usable in the lodge. The others had been blocked with the logs they'd cut. The gunmen in waiting would be positioned strategically around one or, more likely, both doors, and at least two men would be necessary to cover each door. So they were looking for a minimum of four. From his position, Bolan could only see one of the doors. He trained the glasses on it and then swept them from side to side, looking for likely cover.

The rear door was closest to the trees they'd cut down. Jagged stumps stuck up through the snow. Deep drifts, accumulated where the stumps had interfered with the wind currents, arced away from the stumps the same way sandbars bracket an obstruction in the water. Bolan swung the glasses slowly across the stumps, which jutted like the fingers of some giant, buried alive and scratching for air.

As he moved from stump to stump, the warrior let his eyes linger on each one long enough to catch a wayward movement. Every shadow became an assassin for a moment. And, one by one, each one was acquitted. Frustrated, he let the glasses drift back toward the lodge door.

A whisper on the snow behind him caught Bolan's ear, and he turned to see Fontanelli wriggling toward him.

"What the hell are we waiting for?" Fontanelli murmured. "There's no one out here."

"I'm not so sure."

"Have you seen anyone?"

"No..."

"Well, then?"

"They have to be here. We just haven't looked in the right places, that's all."

"Then let's look and get the hell out of here. We're wasting too much time."

Bolan didn't answer as he raised the glasses again. "Come on, where are you, dammit?" He started on the stumps again, then worked his way closer to the door. Bolan was about to give up, when something caught his eye. The moonlight cast a sheen over the snow. Individual snow crystals caught the dim light and reflected it. The surface seemed to shimmer—except in one spot.

About twenty feet down slope from the tree stumps, and at a forty-five-degree angle to the plane of the door, a patch of snow lay flat, its dullness almost lost in the undulating drifts. Looked at directly, it was nearly impossible to tell where the patch started and where it ended. But viewed indirectly, it stood out, the same way a patch of flat white paint would stand out on a wall painted in semigloss. It was the difference in reflectivity, not in color, that gave it away.

If he was right, there would be a second patch elsewhere on the slope, probably no farther from the door, but far enough to the left to give the shooters a chance to cover the opening with a cross fire. The logical place would be a point that gave approximately the same angle of fire.

Bolan searched carefully, first staring directly through the glasses, then focusing his attention on the outer margin of his field of vision, at the very edge of the lens. The play of light and dark was hard on the eyes. Differences so slight were tiring and easily missed. He wasn't even certain he was right. But if he found a second one, he'd know.

Fontanelli tugged on Bolan's coat, and he let go of the glasses long enough to swipe at the impatient hand. Closing his eyes to rest them for a few seconds, he shook his head. He took the glasses away and rubbed his eyes with the cold leather of his gloves. The pressure was soothing, and he scooped some snow and pressed it against his eyelids.

And then he found the second one.

Like the first, it was hard to see, but there was no doubt about it. He pointed it out to Fontanelli.

"So what do we do?"

"Nothing, yet. We have to find the shooters at the front door, too, before we make our move. You stay here. I'll go around front and try to find the others. When I do, I'll call you on the com set."

"Don't take too long."

Bolan moved off without responding. He moved as quickly as caution would permit. The crust of the much-traveled snow was broken in many places, the surface littered with clumps that had melted under the sun and refrozen into rocklike chunks. They kept catching the tips of the snowshoes and slowing him down. At the same time, he had to worry about being seen by the men at the other end of the house.

He wondered whether he and Fontanelli had been spotted on their first circuit, but decided not. They wouldn't have let a clear shot go by, and there was no reason for them to assume they'd get a second chance.

The far side of the house presented a very different set of obstacles to any would-be assassins. Instead of looking down on the lodge, the gunners would be looking up at it. The woods were thicker, offering more potential cover, but Bolan, Novick and Fontanelli had thinned the trees near enough to pose a threat. Large jumbles of broken rock were scattered among the trees, and it hadn't been possible to do anything about them. They offered a veritable maze of nooks and crannies. But the most difficult aspect was the barricade they had fashioned out of logs. Stacked on the patio like cordwood for Paul Bunyan, a wall of thick fir trunks jutted out past the door, parallel to the wall. There was no direct shot.

That narrowed Bolan's search a bit, but the varied terrain offered more possibilities of concealment. As he rounded the far side of the lodge, Bolan slowed up. He knew from his own experience that any motion attracted the eye in so lifeless a landscape. He had to move, but he couldn't afford to move too fast. He dropped lower on the slope, hoping he'd given himself enough leeway to come up behind the gun emplacements.

The warrior stopped among a clump of laurels half buried in the snow. Using the glasses, he quickly skimmed across the open snow, looking for that telltale dullness. His first pass came up empty. He was just about to make a second sweep when the com set came alive in his ear.

"Belasko, can you hear me?" Fontanelli was whispering, and the small, tinny membrane of the earphone gave his voice the sound of an angry insect.

"What's wrong?"

"One of them showed himself. Shall I take him out?"

"No! What do you mean he showed himself?"

"Just that. He stood up all of a sudden. He was under this canvas cover, and he just stood and shook it off. He's closing in on the house right now. The back door."

"Just watch him. If he tries to get in, use your judgment, otherwise sit tight."

"Roger."

Bolan was worried. It looked as if the gunners had gotten tired of waiting. The last thing he wanted was to have the play taken away from him. Using the glasses with a renewed sense of urgency, he started to scrutinize the broken snowfield between the trees and the lodge. Still nothing.

Training the glasses closer in, he slowly swept across the deep shadows thrown by the lodge. As the moon sank lower in the sky, the shadows continued to lengthen. Already they extended nearly a hundred feet in some places, less where the height of the lodge was less imposing. He stopped at the farthest point, where the tip of the chimney cast a thin blue shadow, not as deep as the rest. A dark blob moved toward the house, as if it were descending the chimney.

He thought at first it might be his imagination. Looking more closely, he realized what he was seeing. Bolan shifted the glasses to the roof of the lodge. Two men moved past the chimney, straddling the roof peak and walking on their knees.

"Dominick," he said urgently. "Two men, on the roof."

The earphone crackled for a second, then, "Got 'em."

"You still see your man?"

"Yup."

"All right. I'll take the two on the roof. As soon as you hear the first shot, take out your man, then wait for the other groundhog to pop up."

"Gotcha."

Bolan tucked the microphone back into his pocket. He swung around the Weatherby, then wriggled his shoulders to relax the tension. In the scope, the men on the roof were more clearly outlined. The snow uphill beyond the lodge made for an excellent backdrop.

Bolan zeroed in on the man nearest the edge. The jerky motion of the knee-walking was disconcerting, and the warrior gritted his teeth. He had to make the first shot count. Once it cracked across the snow, the rabbits would all run for cover. If Fontanelli was on the money, he'd be able to take his own man out before the gunman could react to the sound of Bolan's rifle.

As he tightened his finger against the trigger, a sudden flash of light blinded him.

22

A ball of fire erupted behind the lodge. In the brilliant glare, like an orange sun rising out of the earth, the two men on the roof looked like stick figures. Frozen for an instant, they toppled forward, grabbing for the shingles with both hands. Bolan's sight returned slowly. The two gunmen began to move as the light receded.

The fireball was replaced almost immediately by streaks of orange flame. Black, oily smoke curled up into the sky from the tips of the flickering tongues. Bolan squeezed his eyes shut once more, then squinted into the scope. It was like looking at shadows through frosted glass. His vision was blurred, and a bright ball, a dim echo of the original, clouded the center of his focus. Turning his head slightly, he used the peripheral, unaffected by the temporary retinal paralysis, and squeezed.

The Weatherby snapped into his shoulder, and he lost sight of his target for a second. Resighting, he could find only one man. The blinding shock continued to abate. He could see hazily now, and locked in on the second man. This time he watched as the bullet found its mark.

Bolan leaped to his feet and started toward the lodge. A short burst of automatic fire echoed from beyond the lodge, and he recognized the sound of Fontanelli's AR-15. The light from the flames had fallen off sharply, but thick waves of smoke continued to sweep across the roof and gather into a dark cloud. The AR-15 stuttered again, but this time fire was returned. At least one automatic weapon was answering Fontanelli's.

The warrior cleared the last group of boulders and charged into the open snow. So far there was no evidence of movement from inside the lodge. The firebomb had done little structural damage, he guessed, since no debris had flown into the air, but the heat was intense. It was likely that the outside rear of the lodge was a mass of flames, probably still feeding on the accelerant while the wood slowly caught. That would account for the initial flash and the gradual reduction in the amount of light.

As he rounded the corner of the lodge, the front door flew open, and Barry Novick rushed onto the patio, carrying one of the captured M-16s. Bolan called to him, but Novick didn't hear. He charged down the stairs and into the snow, his attention focused on the flames. Bolan called again, but this time a burst of fire from the far side of the structure drowned him out. Novick was floundering in the snow, and lost his balance for an instant.

A slug whistled past Bolan's ear, then he heard the crack of a rifle somewhere behind him. He spun awkwardly, the snowshoes catching in the broken snow. The abrupt change of direction caused him to lose his balance momentarily. He righted himself, then dived to the ground.

Burrowing deeper into the snow, the warrior pressed himself flat, at the same time scanning the field be-

hind him for some sign of the gunman. His eyes had a
tough time adjusting to the gloom. Thin wisps of
smoke had begun to collect in the hollows below the
lodge. Through the haze, as sporadic as a summer fog,
he searched desperately for a sign, some mistake, some
reckless error that would give away the rifleman's lo-
cation.

But there was none. He curled his body to look for
Novick, but the lieutenant had vanished into the
shadows along the side of the house. Bolan was pinned
down, helpless, unless he could find the rifleman. The
gunman knew where he was and no doubt was just
waiting for the warrior to expose himself. Kicking off
his snowshoes, he gripped one like a tennis racket. He
slid the shoe as far to the right as he could manage,
then tilted it upright.

The first shot pinged through the webbing, nearly
knocking it loose from his grip. Bolan had seen the
flash, but not well enough to pinpoint the shooter.
With his eyes rigidly fixed on the general area, he
raised the snowshoe again. The second shot slammed
into the wooden frame, shattering it and sending it
cartwheeling away. Bolan's hand went numb.

But he got what he wanted.

The Executioner swept a shallow depression in the
snow ahead of him. He eased the Weatherby around
cautiously, making sure that he kept below the line of
snow. If the rifleman got a fix on him, there was nowhere to go, and nothing but a heartbeat between life
and sudden death.

Through the scope, he saw a hollow formed by a
fallen tree and a pair of boulders. The flash had come
from the middle of that natural alcove, and the darkness inside it was all but impenetrable. The haze, be-

ginning to drift closer to the ground as the air cooled it down, obscured the sniper still further.

While he waited for something to aim at, Bolan listened to the firefight raging intermittently beyond the lodge. Fontanelli was holding his own, but it sounded as if he were going head to head with two men. If they played it right, they could outflank him. Novick would help a little, but he was still weak, and without snowshoes, he'd be nearly immobile in the deep drifts beyond the lodge.

An abrupt change in the sounds of the battle concerned Bolan. It seemed as if Fontanelli were no longer firing. He couldn't wait longer.

Boring into the eyepiece of the scope, Bolan adjusted his aim slightly, then squeezed. He heard the familiar whine of a ricochet as his bullet struck an unseen outcropping of rock and spun off into the night. He shifted slightly to the right and fired again. This time he heard a thud. It sounded like something soft and wet had been struck, and he realized the bullet had buried itself in the damp wood of the fallen tree.

So far there had been no response from the sniper, and he took the opportunity to load a couple of cartridges into the magazine. A dull thud, followed by a sharp whoosh of air, made the Executioner turn his head. The sudden pop high above him was followed immediately by a blaze of brilliant white light. Bolan glanced up in surprise as the flare hovered overhead, its frail parachute a round white cloud two feet above it.

The blinding light flooded the outer portion of the niche where the sniper lay hidden. A splash of dark green, out of place in that snow-filled crevice, was all

Bolan needed. He aimed high and to the left, squeezing the Weatherby's trigger. Through the scope, he caught a bright red flower blooming and dying, all in a single instant.

The gunman pitched facedown into the snow, his rifle parallel to his lifeless body. The flare sputtered like a small engine running out of gas, then began to grow dim. A moment later, it drifted all the way down, now little more than a dying ember. It winked out in the snow with a single hiss.

Bolan groped in the snow for the snowshoes, then strapped them back on. The one he'd used as bait had been shot through. Its shattered rim flopped badly, but the webbing was still intact, and any help in the snow was better than nothing.

He scrambled out of the snow and raced toward the patio. As Bolan drew within ten yards of the lodge, he heard another flare go up. It cracked open like an egg full of light and drifted slowly across the snowfield up the mountain. A plume of smoke drifted off at a forty-five-degree angle as the parachute slowly sailed off on the wind.

Ducking in along the tumbled logs that reinforced the base of the building, Bolan sprinted toward the flames. He reached the rear of the lodge just as Novick ducked around the corner. The flare pistol in his hand was broken open, and he struggled to get another shell in. As a spray of lead from the hillside chipped at the wooden wall just above the detective's head, Bolan dragged him down into the snow. Novick landed hard on his injured side.

"What the hell's wrong with you?" Bolan shouted. "What are you doing out here?"

Novick groaned as he tried to sit up. Through clenched teeth, he said, "When the bomb went off, I ran to the back wall. It blew off the boards we nailed over one of the second-story windows. I could see that Fontanelli was pinned down. What else could I do?"

"All right, all right. Get back inside and don't open the door."

"What about the fire?"

"It'll have to wait."

"Tell that to Mrs. Fontanelli. She's hysterical." He gasped as he twisted his body to get up. With one hand on the pile of logs, he hauled himself to his feet. They both heard the shout at the same time, as Roseanne dashed off the patio, her son in her arms.

"Go back," Novick shouted, limping back along the wall. He called over his shoulder to Bolan and tossed the flare pistol to him. "You'll probably need this."

Bolan snatched it out of the air and crammed it into his pocket. He sprinted toward the back corner. As he drew close, the heat of the flames singed his skin. He had to move away from the building to avoid the worst of the fire. The brilliant orange light shimmered as the wind swept rags of black smoke around the corner.

Over the crackle of the flames, he could hear the steady drip of water as the heat rose and melted the snow on the roof. A large semicircle of brown earth marked the perimeter of the blast. The soil looked sticky and loose where melted snow had turned it to mud.

Roseanne's shrieking slowly faded as Novick hustled her back into the lodge. The snow melt from the roof had begun to run down the wall, soaking the burning wood and extinguishing the flames in long vertical strips. Bolan watched the flare continue to drift away and, when it finally died, he started up the hill.

Thirty yards from the lodge, he found a shallow depression and scrambled in. He tried to raise Fontanelli on the com set, but all he got was a burst of static. He wiggled the wire to the earphone, and Fontanelli's voice faded in and out, as if it had been cut into strips and only odd-numbered bits were fed through.

Bolan jammed the wire up into the earphone. The connection was better, but the signal was weak. Fontanelli sounded as if he were on the other side of the mountain, at the limit of the unit's range. When he covered his other ear, Bolan could hear well enough to carry on a conversation.

"Are you all right?" he asked.

"I'm okay, but my gun's jammed."

"How many are there?"

"Two."

"Where?"

"Right where you guessed. There were two guys under each tarp. I nailed one, and another one charged the lodge and set off the incendiary. I don't know what happened to him."

"Hang tough. Don't use your handgun unless you have to. Once you do, they'll know you're in trouble."

"You'd better hurry."

Bolan dropped to his stomach and started up the slope. The snowshoes hampered him, and he stopped to kick them off. He knew he was sacrificing some mobility if he had to run, but time was short. He crawled toward the nearer of the two tarps, now almost invisible as the moon disappeared behind the mountain. The stars overhead sparkled brightly, but their cold light was useless to him. He had only one flare. Unless he flushed one of the men, it was as useless as the stars.

The tarp was fifty yards uphill. As he drew closer, he could just distinguish it from the surrounding snow. Its off-white color looked like a faint shadow, where no shadow should lie. It was nearly ten feet square and lay so flat it didn't betray the presence of the man beneath it. He could shoot it full of holes and run out of ammo long before he found his target.

Twenty yards closer in, he saw the tarp ripple as the hidden man changed his position. With ten yards to go, he was sure. He got to his knees and brought his rifle around. Drawing a bead on a bulge under the left half, he pumped a slug through the canvas. The tarp bucked wildly, and Bolan fired again. This time the movement grew more subdued, then stopped altogether, like a windup toy whose spring had run down.

He had to reload while he could. The second tarp was fifty yards to his right. Dropping back to his stomach, he rested the Weatherby across his forearms and snaked through the snow. His weight kept cracking the crust, and the soft snow underneath slipped away from his knees and elbows. Like running in loose sand, it took twice the energy for half the speed.

The snow just below him suddenly spouted into the air. The bark of an M-16 jerked his head back toward the lodge. He curled into a ball, grabbed on to his rifle and spun in a half circle. Another burst kicked pellets of snow into his face.

He shouldered the Weatherby and waited for the gunner to reveal himself. A third burst ripped past his ear. The muzzle-flash was dim, and came from the far corner of the lodge. The firebomber had found him. He fired, and rolling over once, sighted through the scope. The muzzle flashed again and Bolan sent his two last rounds right through the heart of the flames. He heard a groan, then the crash of metal on stone.

Lying on his back, he stuck his hand into his pocket for the box of ammo. The tarp was on his left now, and he glanced at it as his hand closed on the cardboard box. As he grabbed three cartridges, the tarp began to move. It rose up and hovered like a cartoon ghost for an instant, then fell away as the man beneath it charged into the open.

Bolan clawed at his jacket, but his weight pinned it to his body. The flare pistol slipped out of his pocket as he raised his hip to get at the Desert Eagle. His only option was the flare gun. The gunman barreled straight toward him, his M-16 up and ready. Bolan pointed the flare pistol and fired.

The flare slammed into the charging man, then went off with a loud pop. The gunner screamed as the phosphorus ignited. He clutched at his stomach, but it was too late to remove the embedded flare. A cone of white light speared out of his gut as he toppled, his hands grasping desperately at the white-hot flare. His hands turned bright red, and Bolan could see the finger bones outlined in their flesh. The gunner's body curled around the searing heat and he toppled into the snow.

23

The last flame guttered out, and Bolan gave the blackened wood a final shot with the fire extinguisher. Above him, inside, Fontanelli tacked the last board in place over the damaged window. The light disappeared as the board slid home. Fontanelli drove the last nail home with the determination of a mortician nailing a coffin shut.

The damage to the lodge, although extensive, appeared to be superficial. Bolan lugged the extinguisher toward the back door, then used it to rap on the heavy wood. Novick jerked the door open, and he stepped inside.

"All finished?" the detective asked.

Bolan nodded.

"Then let's get going," Fontanelli said.

"You're not going to leave us here?" Roseanne was incredulous. Her voice trembled, and she looked from Bolan to her husband, then back to Bolan. She looked like someone meeting identical twins for the first time.

"Barry will be with you and Anthony," her husband reminded her.

"But—"

"Look, neither one of us can get Junior back alone. Maybe, just maybe, Belasko and I can swing it together. We can't drag you along, and neither of us can stay here. So..."

"But maybe the police—"

"Fuck the police," Fontanelli shouted. "Don't you understand? The goddamned sheriff was in on the kidnapping. How the hell can we trust anybody but ourselves?"

Roseanne dropped her head. When she spoke, her voice had lost its tremble. But it had also lost its life. She sounded like a mourner at a funeral. "You're right. Of course you are. It's just that..."

Fontanelli knelt beside her chair. "Rosie, if there were any other way... but there isn't."

"I know," she said. "I guess that's what scares me. Dom, I'm terrified. Terrified I'll never see my son again, terrified I'll lose you, too. Then what will I do?"

He patted her knee. "I'll be back. I promise you, I'll be back. And Junior will be with me. Just hang on a little longer, that's all I ask. When this is all over, we'll go away somewhere, the four of us."

"Where can we go? How can we run? They'll always be after us."

"Not if I kill them all." She raised her head, and Fontanelli chucked her under the chin. "I know what you're thinking. But it's not like that. This is different. This is real and it's personal. No nightmares, no flashbacks. When this is done, and I swear to you it will be, then it's really over. For good."

Roseanne shook her head as if she understood. But Bolan knew, and he thought Fontanelli also knew, that she *didn't* understand. But she wanted to, and for her husband's sake she would pretend.

Bolan led the way to the Blazer. Neither man was in the mood for conversation. When the garage trap slammed home, Bolan jerked the driver's door open and took a quick inventory of the armament. There was plenty of ammo, and they had backups for everything except the Weatherby and Fontanelli's scoped Sauer.

The block of plastique Bolan had salvaged from the Caravan sat in a cardboard box. In a canvas bag next to it, a lantern battery, some wire and the detonator kept company with a half dozen old grenades and the flare pistol with its last three flares. If they needed anything heavier, they'd have to improvise.

Bolan started the Blazer, and Fontanelli opened the garage door manually. When the 4X4 rolled out into the snow, Fontanelli closed the door again and snapped a heavy padlock to keep it closed. Bolan gunned the engine while he waited, and when Fontanelli climbed in, he threw it in gear before the door closed.

As Bolan drove, he let his mind sort through the past few days. He wanted to make sure he hadn't overlooked anything. Their first destination was the sheriff's office. Neither man expected to find Dominick Junior in a cell, but if the sheriff was there, they'd start with him. If not, they'd squeeze whoever they found until they got what they wanted.

The trip went smoothly. The road was still snow-covered, and though it had been plowed, the steady winds had created new drifts, some as deep as eighteen inches. The sky was clear, but the temperature was dropping steadily. A weather report had predicted new snow but, as usual, the forecaster had played it safe. He'd been noncommittal about when or how much.

The road was unlighted. At three in the morning, they weren't expecting any traffic. Fontanelli stared out his window. His outward calm, Bolan knew, was deceptive. No man in his situation could help but be tied in knots. Staring at the snow-covered landscape was less a sightseer's fascination than an attempt at self-hypnosis. With the fingers of one hand, Fontanelli tapped a steady rhythm on the padded dash. It was the only sound, and the only movement, he made.

WALTON WAS DESERTED. The streets, lighted by staggered lamps, were more like tunnels than thoroughfares, with the deep snow plowed into mounds on either curb. The main street, lined with shops on both sides, featured the only parking meters in town, and half of them were completely buried under the plowed snow.

Like most small towns, Walton was usually a peaceful place. The windows of the stores weren't hidden behind rolling metal doors, or locked behind steel grids. As the Blazer moved down the main street, Bolan could see the vehicle reflected in the shop windows on his side of the street. The windows themselves were dark, and the neon signs were unlighted.

The sheriff's office was at the opposite end of town, sharing Walton city hall with the mayor and the town council. Bolan pulled the Blazer into a narrow alley about half a block from the city hall. The alley had been plowed, but the walls of the buildings pressed in so close on both sides there was barely enough room to open both doors. He rammed the Blazer through to a small parking lot in front of a row of old garages.

Shutting off the engine, he reached into the back for one of the M-16s, slipped several clips into his jacket pocket and got out of the vehicle. He closed the door softly, then moved to the front of the 4X4 to wait for Fontanelli. He watched the man through the windshield. Fontanelli took several deep breaths, like a man preparing for his last attempt at a world record. His lips moved, and Bolan turned away. He didn't know whether Fontanelli was just talking to himself or praying, but either way, it seemed inappropriate to spy on him. Bolan turned back when he heard the door latch click.

The rear alley connected to the back of city hall. It was dark, and they moved quickly into the final stretch. The two men broke into a slow trot, their feet thumping on the snow. As they broke out of the alley into the municipal parking lot, Bolan held up his hand. He crouched behind the end of a peeling picket fence.

The rear of the building looked deserted. The back wall was a slab of brick and tinted glass, unbroken except by a single flight of concrete stairs that climbed parallel to the wall to a landing. An iron railing, painted dull green, served as a banister and surrounded the six-foot-square landing at waist level. In the center of the landing, a metal door, windowless and painted the same green, sat under a single bare red bulb.

The parking lot was deserted. Two cruisers for the sheriff's department were parked in the far corner, and private cars occupied half of the cleared asphalt. In the three stories of tinted glass, not a single light was visible. Beyond the lot, another row of garages—this one facing away from city hall—formed a solid barrier.

"Looks clear," Bolan whispered, then eased around the fence and sprinted for the concrete stairs. He kept to a crouch and skidded to a halt at the base of the stairway. He paused to listen for a moment, then waved Fontanelli on. Taking the stairs cautiously, Bolan stopped on the landing for a second, then placed his ear to the cold sheet metal. He heard nothing. The knob turned easily at his touch. The latch snicked softly, and Bolan pulled. The door swung open without a sound.

He found himself staring down a long hallway, glass partitions lining either side. Through the greenish glass, he could make out the contours of filing cabinets and desks. A single red bulb, mounted in the ceiling at the middle of the passage, was the only light.

Bolan slipped through the doorway and waited for Fontanelli to join him. "Ever been here before?"

"A few times," he whispered, "but never here. Just at the front desk."

"Where's the jail?"

"In the basement. I guess we can get there through here, but I'm not sure."

"Let's give it a shot," Bolan said.

He started down the hall, keeping below the level of the glass. When he reached the midpoint, he called Fontanelli forward with a jerk of his hand, then raised his head to peek through the glass. He could see very little beyond the panels. Several red lamps, like the one above him, were scattered across the ceiling, but no other light burned in the room.

He continued down the passage and found himself at an intersection. The warrior peered around the corner and down another corridor similar to the one he'd just traversed. He could see all the way to the far wall, to another green metal door positioned under a red-and-white Exit sign.

Straight ahead, a third door, just like the other two, seemed like the only way to go. Fontanelli slipped past him and dashed to the door. After listening carefully, he tried the knob. When he pushed the door open a crack, a sliver of white light fell on the floor. But the room beyond seemed to be totally silent.

Bolan joined him, and they slipped through the opening. They found another hallway, this one shorter. Instead of the glass partitions, this one had solid walls, broken by two doors on the left and one on the right. All the doors were closed, and plastic signs were mounted over each, identifying the occupant by name and title.

At the end of the hall, an opening to the right looked promising. Bolan moved ahead, and found a flight of concrete stairs leading down. "This must be it," he whispered.

"It has to be," Fontanelli answered.

Bolan took the point. The stairs were dark. At the bottom, a right turn led into the holding tanks and a small cell block. Bolan peeked in, but under a dim, shielded bulb, the tank and the cells were all empty. To the left, a door with a wired-glass window allowed a block of light through.

On the far side, two men playing cards wore the brown shirt and pants of a deputy. Neither had been with Greenway the day before. Bolan secured his grip on the M-16. He didn't intend to hurt these men, but they had no way of knowing it. He had to be prepared for the worst.

Fontanelli knelt and reached for the knob. Bolan steeled himself. With a nod of his head, he gave his companion the go. The knob turned, and Bolan planted a boot dead center. The door flew back with a bang. As he charged into the room, both deputies started to rise, the cards flying in every direction.

"Don't move!" Bolan barked.

One of the deputies jerked his hand. Bolan lashed out with the muzzle of the M-16, catching him just above the elbow. The man howled and doubled over in agony.

"Where's my son?" Fontanelli hissed.

The other deputy said, "How the hell do I know? I don't even know who you are."

"You will," Fontanelli snarled. "I promise you that." he took a step forward, but Bolan blocked his path.

"Where's the sheriff?" he asked, holding his companion back with one arm.

"He's not here."

"I can see that. Where is he?"

"Gone huntin', at least that's what he told me."

"Where?"

"I don't know. Hell, *he's* the sheriff. I'm just a deputy. He doesn't tell me anything."

"If you *were* sheriff, where do you think *you'd* go hunting?"

"I know where he is," the injured man said, groaning.

Fontanelli swung his gun around and pressed the muzzle against the deputy's chest. "Where?"

"I got to show you. You'll never find it, otherwise."

"Get your coat."

24

Fontanelli herded the deputy into the back room. "Pick your favorite cell."

The deputy turned to glare at him. "Real comedian, aren't you?"

"I used to be," Fontanelli replied. "But somehow, having my son kidnapped hasn't done much for my sense of humor."

"Look, I didn't have anything to do with that. You gotta believe me."

"I do. That's why you're still alive."

Fontanelli opened the cell door and bowed graciously, waving the deputy inside. As the man stepped past him, he snared the heavy key ring jangling from the deputy's belt. "Take your cuffs and put one on."

The deputy did as he was told. "Now, lock the other around the bunk." Glumly the deputy fingered the dangling cuff. "Now," Fontanelli snapped.

"Look," the deputy argued. "I'm not going anywhere."

"I know," Fontanelli said, his grim smile convincing the deputy that argument was futile. The cuff snapped home, and Fontanelli checked both ends. The cuffs were secure. "Where's the key?"

The deputy reached into his shirt pocket and tossed it to him. Fontanelli caught the key then backed out of the cell. He closed the cell door, locked it and turned to leave.

"Fontanelli . . ."

He turned, and the deputy said, "Rawls didn't have anything to do with it, either. I mean we knew, but...hey, I'm sorry, man. I hope your kid's all right."

"You'd better." Fontanelli walked out of the cell block.

Out front, Bolan had Rawls ready. The deputy wore his uniform coat and had his hands cuffed behind him. Fontanelli headed for the stairs, and Bolan urged the deputy after him. The three men climbed the stairs and walked down the long, silent corridor to the back door. Once outside, the two men flanked the deputy, Fontanelli linking arms with the handcuffed man.

"If you're thinking about making a run for it, don't."

Rawls nodded. "I don't want trouble. I just want to come out of this alive."

"Don't worry about it," Bolan told him. "Just do as you're told."

They double-timed down the alley, Rawls running awkwardly because his manacled arms disturbed his balance. Fontanelli climbed into the rear of the Blazer, then Bolan helped Rawls into the front bucket. Getting behind the wheel, he said, "Where to?"

"It's an old mining camp up in the mountains. About an hour from here."

Fontanelli leaned forward. "If you're thinking about taking us on a snipe hunt, buddy, I strongly suggest that you reconsider. If you don't take us to the sheriff and my son, I'm going to take you apart with this rifle, a pound at a time. Do you understand?"

Rawls nodded, but it wasn't good enough for Fontanelli. "Say it," he whispered. "Say you understand."

Rawls swallowed with some difficulty. "I understand."

"Good."

They were the only vehicle on the road. As Walton fell behind, its few lights began to fade, and ten minutes later they were in total darkness. Leaning forward to look at the sky, Bolan could see a few hard points of light where a handful of stars cut through the glare of the dash lights. As they sped higher, even those disappeared. Stopping for a moment, Bolan rolled down his window and leaned out. A leaden pall was beginning to move in, the mass behind it solid. The black turned to dark, solid gray.

As the front approached from the west, carrying moist air from the Pacific, the mountains forced it higher and higher. The leading edge of the clouds seemed to tumble over some unseen obstacle, boiling like a breaker hitting the beach.

"It doesn't look good," Bolan muttered.

"How much longer?" Fontanelli asked.

"Half hour or so." Rawls sounded nervous when he answered. "I've only been there twice. I didn't drive either time, so I'm not exactly sure. I know we're heading in the right direction, though."

"Can't you make this thing go any faster?" Fontanelli asked.

Bolan shook his head. "Not if you want to get there." The 4X4 was slipping on the curves as it was. Bolan held the needle at a solid fifty, braking only for the worst turns. The road wound its lazy way, curling back on itself every so often, each time snaking a little higher into the mountains. On either side of the road, dense forest swept away as far as they could see.

"We got to go through Big Horn Pass up ahead. About a mile. On the other side of the pass, you got to look for a road. Then we travel that for ten miles or so. That's where we make the turnoff. There's a sign, I think, but it's just plywood. It might even be buried."

Bolan drummed his fingers on the wheel. He was getting impatient, and Fontanelli was ready to explode. The road, a long upward sweep, zigzagged just enough to slow descending cars. A notch in the mountain loomed above them. As they drew close, a sign identified the pass and gave its altitude as 11,201 feet above sea level. The dark gray beyond the pass was a stark contrast to the pale snow on either slope. The forest had thinned considerably in the last couple of miles as they approached the tree line.

The Blazer rushed through the notch and leveled off. The road undulated over a desolate plateau, as if to give traffic time to catch its breath. Ahead, another steep ascent would carry it still higher. Bolan opened it up, pushing the needle to sixty.

"Just over the rise, you got to slow up," Rawls cautioned. "We're getting close."

Bolan eased off the gas as they rode over the gentle hill, then let the Blazer coast down the far side.

"It's on the right, somewhere in here." Rawls sounded as if he were talking to himself. "There, stop, right there." Bolan leaned forward. A stake and the warped and faded edge of a piece of plywood just peeked over the top of the snow.

Bolan kicked the emergency brake on. He dropped to the roadway and walked to the turnoff. Under the blown snow, he could see evidence that something had passed through recently. He knelt and brushed at the snow with a gloved hand. The top crust cracked, and the fluffy snow underneath gave way readily. Two inches down, his fingers encountered a second hard crust. He didn't have to see clearly to recognize the tread marks of the half-track.

He sprinted back to the Blazer. "How far in?" he asked the deputy.

Rawls shrugged. "A mile or a mile and a half, I guess."

Fontanelli leaned forward. "We going to make it in this thing?"

"I think so," Bolan said. "We'll have to walk partway, anyhow."

The Blazer rocked and rolled, sometimes scraping the snow with its undercarriage, sometimes leaning so far to one side or the other it seemed about to capsize. Fontanelli's anxiety mounted geometrically, seeming to double every hundred yards or so. His hands rapped the back of the front seat nervously.

Bolan killed the lights, and they continued on another three hundred yards in darkness. The wind grabbed at the Blazer, trying to wrest control from Bolan's straining arms. At the next gap in the trees, he spun the wheel. The Blazer jounced down off the elevated roadbed and lumbered into the underbrush. Branches lashed the sides and snatched at the fenders and suspension.

"End of the line," Bolan announced. He killed the engine and dumped the ignition key in his pocket. "How many men does he have with him?"

"I don't know, honest to God. Two deputies, for sure. But I don't know who else. He made a couple phone calls before he left, though. If that means anything.''

''We'll have to leave you here,'' Bolan said. Fontanelli already had his snowshoes on. He slung the Sauer over his shoulder and hefted his AR-15. His pockets bulged with ammunition, and the canvas sack with the grenades dangled from his left forearm.

Bolan cuffed Rawls to the steering column, then reached under the dash and jerked the fuse pack free, disabling the Blazer's electrical system. Tucking it into his pocket, he said, ''Just in case you decide to take up the horn in your spare time.''

''You don't miss a trick, do you?'' Rawls asked. His tone was equal parts sarcasm and admiration.

Bolan grabbed his own weapons and piled them on the hood, then returned for his snowshoes. Once they were belted in place, he arranged his gear and stepped to the front of the Blazer, where Fontanelli waited impatiently. ''Let's go,'' he said.

They hadn't gone more than a hundred yards when the first faint glimmer of light appeared through the trees ahead. Fontanelli broke into a trot and Bolan had to run him down. The last thing either man wanted was to tip their hand at this late date. So far all they knew for sure was that Rawls had taken them to the sheriff. Whether Dominick Junior was being held by the sheriff, and if so whether he was being held here, remained to be seen. Fontanelli couldn't contain his anxiety, and he resented Bolan's attempt to rein him in.

But Bolan was adamant. ''Look, if your son's here we can't afford to give up the only advantage we have. If they know we're coming, you're putting his life in jeopardy. I know you don't want that, but it's a fact you have to face. At best, they'll whisk him out of here . . . and you already know the downside.''

Fontanelli shook his head in frustration. ''We're so damned close.''

''Not close enough.''

Bolan moved ahead, aware of the angry scrape of Fontanelli's snowshoes right on his heels. As the light grew brighter, the wind picked up in intensity. It began to snow, which Bolan thought might tip the scales their way a little. No doubt the sheriff already felt secure. Bad weather would enhance that feeling and, just possibly, encourage him to relax his guard.

The road started to descend slightly, and the light loomed above them, on the far side of a shallow bowl in the mountain. The sparse trees offered little cover and less protection from the growling winds. Snow swirled around them, a hard, cold snow that reflected the dropping temperature.

As far as Rawls knew, the road they followed was the only one in or out of the abandoned camp. If a guard had been posted, he was likely somewhere directly in front of them. Bolan drifted off the road and found the going in the drifts among the trees no more difficult.

They were nearly at the bottom of the bowl when Bolan spotted the guard. A Ford Bronco, its engine throbbing softly, sat across the road, almost dead center at the bottom of the depression. The dark blue 4X4 stood out against the snow, and its windshield reflected one of two lights glowing in a cabin halfway up the far side. It was the reflected light that gave it away.

Bolan pointed out the Bronco, placing a hand on Fontanelli's arm to restrain him. ''You wait here.''

"Why?"

"Because one of us has to get out of here if they spot us."

"Then let me go."

"No. Dominick, you're too close to this. You're not thinking straight."

Reluctantly he agreed. Bolan moved off in a wide circle that would bring him around behind the Bronco. He kept one eye on the cabin as he closed in on the chugging vehicle. He could see the exhaust, just visible as it drifted up behind the dark blue paint.

As he narrowed the gap, he was startled by a sudden burst of red, then realized the guard had accidentally stepped on the brake, perhaps rearranging his position inside the Bronco. He noticed that the Bronco's rear window was fogged over. The sentry must be using the heater only enough to warm the interior, then shutting it down.

He could hope the side windows were just as foggy, but couldn't bank on it. Dropping to his stomach, Bolan slid forward, his legs bent at the knees to raise the tips of the snowshoes off the ground. Without being able to use his feet, the going was slow. He had the Beretta in his pocket. In a pinch, he could use the M-16, but if he had to shoot, he hoped it would be with enough advance notice to permit use of the silenced pistol.

Close enough to the bumper to touch it with the tips of his fingers, he was startled once more by a burst of red. It killed whatever hope he had that the guard might have nodded off. The engine gunned, and Bolan heard the compressor begin to whir. The guard had turned the heater on again.

Bolan couldn't decide which side to hit. If either door was open, it was most likely the driver's side. If he tried the other door and it was locked, he lost his advantage. On the other hand, if he approached the driver's door, the man might see him before he was ready. He could just turn the Beretta loose and take the sentry out without warning, but that seemed too cold-blooded. It was possible, although remotely, that some of the deputies had been misled by Greenway and acted out of a sense of duty.

The internal debate seemed endless, but it took only seconds. In the end, he did the only thing he could do. Taking the Beretta out of his coat, he hauled himself to his feet. Keeping below the mirror's line of sight, he crawled along the driver's side. Just behind the door, he stood abruptly and rapped on the glass with the muzzle of the Beretta. Through the half-misted glass, he saw the wide eyes of the surprised guard, who raised his hands in a spasmodic surrender. Bolan backed off a step and gestured for the door to be opened.

The lock clicked and Bolan thought for a moment the guard had changed his mind. But the door swung open, spilling yellow light on the snow.

"Get out," Bolan whispered. "Slowly."

25

Now they knew the odds. Twelve men waited for them. Twelve men and a little boy. The guard was left bound and gagged in the back of the Bronco. The engine was still running, and the heat on low. Bolan snagged the walkie-talkie off the front seat and tucked it under his arm. If the sheriff tried to raise the guard, they would have to move fast.

The cabin was secure, but not impregnable. Its rear was set right into the hillside, leaving only three walls to be defended. A shaft under the cabin floor dropped straight to the main shaft of the mine, which ran into the hill on a right angle. The mouth of the mine was about one hundred yards to the left of the cabin. Two other buildings, a stable for the mules that had been used to haul ore cars in and out of the mine, and a storage shed, lay within twenty yards of the cabin.

It was a tactical nightmare. Two men... and two entrances. If they split up, each would be seriously outgunned. If they went together, one entrance would have to be left unguarded. And what could go in could also go out.

"There's only one way to do it," Bolan said. "We have to block the mine entrance and hit them from the front. We can't block the cabin, and we don't want to risk it anyway, because Junior is somewhere inside."

"Screw that! It'll take too long. I say we hit them hard, right now, and worry about it later."

"Dominick, listen to me. If they get your son out of there, we might never find him again. Do you want to take that chance?"

"If we hit them hard enough, it won't matter. And we won't need a second chance."

"And if we don't...?"

Fontanelli walked away from the Bronco. He stood with his back to Bolan, staring off at the mountain. The storm raged around him, and the landscape was little more than a blur, a vague, forbidding presence that threatened to swallow everything and everyone that mattered. He knew Bolan was right, and he hated it. Used to shaping the world, twisting it, turning it, tearing it to pieces and reassembling it in a way that pleased him, he didn't want to accept this new and more threatening reality.

But he had to.

"Okay."

They cut across the underbrush, approaching the mine at an angle and moving as fast as prudence allowed. It was just an hour before sunrise. The storm would be at its height by then, but the dawn would still make their task more difficult.

Bolan approached the mouth of the mine. As he drew closer, he heard voices in sleepy conversation. Someone yawned, trying to talk through it and garbling his words.

"Maybe so," another man answered. "I just don't like those guys from New York. I don't trust them, either."

"Hell," the yawner said, "I couldn't care less. I make a little on the side, get myself that new pickup and nobody cares where I got the money. What's the big deal?''

"The big deal is these guys don't like witnesses."

"Witnesses, hell. We ain't witnesses, Randolph. We're fuckin' accomplices."

"Even so."

"Don't worry about it. Jesus, you sound like an old lady."

"That's just 'cause I want to live to be an old man."

"Like I don't, right?"

"It's different for you. You don't have a family."

"Damn right. That's askin' for trouble. If Fontanelli didn't have a family, his nuts wouldn't be in the wringer now."

"You better hope he don't hear you talk like that."

"What, talk? Hell, he swaps himself for the kid, he's smoke, man. History. Vapor."

"If this is so easy, how come they need us in the first place?"

"Why don't you give it a rest, Randolph? Christ, you're starting to get on my nerves."

"I need a drink."

Bolan slipped along the outer face of the mine during the exchange, hoping they talked long enough to get him close. By the time Randolph shut up, the Executioner was just fifteen feet from the mouth of the shaft. By the hollow sound of their voices, he guessed the two men were at least ten feet inside, possibly even more. Bolan unbelted his snowshoes and stood them on end against the rock face.

He closed his fingers over the plastique. This was going to take some doing. He withdrew the Beretta and edged closer to the lip. The arch of raw stone yawned darkly, as if about to swallow the broken rock piled on either side like cookie crumbs on a kid's mouth. A flicker of dirty orange light rose and fell on the snow just outside the entrance. Bolan guessed they had a small fire going for heat. He could touch the stone now, and reached for it to steady himself.

He was in midstride when the walkie-talkie crackled. "Brady, wake up. You there? Brady?" Even distorted by the tinny speaker, the voice was recognizable as that of Walt Greenway. The sound had a peculiar echo, and he realized he was hearing the unit in his own pocket and a second one, inside the mine.

Greenway barked again, then held off for Brady's reply. Bolan realized Brady wasn't going to answer— he was bound and gagged in the Bronco. Bolan held his breath, waiting to see what Greenway would do.

Randolph's companion in the mine laughed. "Brady's gonna get reamed for sure. Walt's gonna chew him out from now till Easter."

"How come he doesn't answer, I wonder?"

"Asshole's asleep. What else?"

Bolan heard the scrape of a match on stone. A moment later the acrid stench of a cheap cigar wafted out of the mine. "Take that damn thing outside, would you? You know I'm allergic."

"Shit, is there anything you aren't allergic to?"

"Pussy," Randolph replied.

"How would you *know*?" The other man laughed.

"One of these days, Charlie, I'm gonna get tired of your shit."

"Don't hit me. I'm allergic." Charlie laughed, and the sound drifted toward Bolan. Under the laughter, he heard boots on the stone floor of the mine. Bolan pressed back against the rock, shifting the Beretta for a better grip. A cloud of bluish smoke drifted out of the entrance. The boots stopped for a second, then Randolph said, "All the way out, Charlie."

The feet started to move again, and Bolan tensed. He saw the tip of one boot, then a hat brim. Another stride brought Charlie halfway out of the mine. Bolan wriggled his fingers. The man took another step, turning to look back over his left shoulder. "Maybe we ought to—"

The gunshot jerked his head back to the right.

"The hell was that?" he said. He took a step toward Bolan, then realized he was staring straight at a man with a gun. A second shot cracked back toward the cabin and Bolan moved, trying to decide who had fired and why.

Charlie wore a Python on his hip, and his hand fumbled at the holster. "Randolph, look out!" he shouted. Bolan fired. The spit of the 93-R was swallowed by the yawning mouth. The 9 mm slug caught Charlie high on the shoulder, and his arm went limp. He lowered his head for a charge, even as the impact of the bullet spun him halfway around. Bolan fired again and dived to the ground as Randolph sprinted toward him.

Charlie's Python cleared his holster and fell from his hand in a single motion. He sprawled backward on the wet stone. The gun went off with a deafening roar. Bolan rolled to his left and swung the Beretta around. Randolph appeared from the darkness of the mine, like an image materializing on a developing photograph. He was charging at full speed, and Bolan hit him with his first shot. Randolph's Winchester carbine fired once, then dropped to the stone.

Randolph seemed to stumble. Bolan held fire and watched as the man pitched forward, both hands reaching for the same dark spot on his coat. The fingers twitched, then seemed to get tangled together as he fell on them. His elbows cracked on the stone, and he lay still. His Stetson, pushed back by its brim, slid off his head and fell sideways into a patch of melting snow.

A single drop of water from the ceiling echoed as it plopped into a shallow pool in the stone floor. Then it was silent. Bolan dashed back to the mouth of the mine. He stared into the darkness back toward the cabin, but the same dim light glowed. It was deathly still.

But something had changed, and he sensed it. Running back to the mine entrance, he stooped to grab a flashlight from Randolph's pocket. Without breaking stride, he clicked the light on and played it ahead of him. The darkness ahead swallowed the light, and he swung it from side to side to track the walls. The beam fractured on the uneven face of the rock, sometimes glinting where it caught on a sharp edge from a pick.

The sound of his feet on the damp floor kept rushing back at him, and then swept away into the darkness ahead and behind him. It was as if he were the only thing alive. To his left, old rails, their ties long since rotted, lay rusting in the dark water. Overhead, thick oak beams, some bowed with age, strained to hold up the stone roof.

As Bolan drew near the place he judged the cabin to be, he slowed. Moving cautiously now, he used the light to examine both walls for several yards ahead, moving along only when satisfied that they were solid. Brady had told him there was an entrance to the cabin from the shaft, but he wasn't sure what he was looking for.

Checking another ten yards, he still found no sign. Then the rails curved to the left, and he played the light along the rust-covered steel. An upturned ore carrier, two of its wheels missing, leaned against the wall. Beyond it, a stack of ties, five or six deep, formed a rough cube, like giant Lincoln Logs.

Bolan moved still more closely, feeling his way along the right face of the shaft as he examined the left in the torch light. The light flickered and grew dim for a second, then returned before fading completely. Bolan rapped the flashlight with the heel of his hand and the light returned, brighter than before.

Playing the light along the wall beyond the stacked ties, the irregular circle suddenly vanished. It took him a second to realize he had found a hole in the face of the shaft. He stepped around the ties and found himself staring into a cubical chamber carved out of the living rock. Taller than the shaft itself, it appeared to be fifteen feet on an edge, and in the far corner, a flight of wooden steps led up through the ceiling.

Bolan crossed the rock-littered floor and trained the light up through the square hole in the ceiling. The stairs zigzagged back and forth, with a landing every twenty feet or so. The stairs continued beyond the reach of the beam of light. The wooden stairs were damp, and the steps themselves seemed to give a little under his weight. He moved cautiously, trying to keep silent, and mindful that a misstep might alert the men somewhere above him.

The stairway was anchored into the stone, braced with rough-hewed timbers. A trickle of water ran down the walls, dripping on the wood here and there, and the pools picked up the flashlight's beam and bounced it off the walls. Bolan kept a rough count of the steps. At fifty, he was about thirty-five feet off the floor of the shaft below. The walls still towered above him, and he could see nothing at the end of the flashlight's dim finger.

Step by step, flight by flight, he climbed higher. Finally a moment that he thought might never come—far above him, perhaps thirty or forty feet, he finally saw the top of the stairs. Rough timbers covered the top of the shaft, their undersides glistening with moisture. At the final landing, he stopped to listen. The last flight was longer than the others, running twenty-five steps to a small landing. From there, a wooden ladder ran straight up the rock for nearly ten feet. Just above the ladder, on a line with it, was a wooden door.

Faint light fell through narrow cracks between the timbers, banding the wet rock with silver streaks. Bolan checked his rifle, removed the safety and gripped the weapon in his right hand. He steadied his climb up the ladder with his left, leaning into the wall to keep his balance. With his head just below the timbers, he waited, his breath held for a long minute. The drip of water down the shaft below him was the only sound he heard.

The door was knobless, and opened and closed only by a rusted handle screwed into the wood. He pushed on the door. It creaked softly, then swung open a few inches. There was still no noise from the room beyond. Peering through the gap, all he could see was some rough wooden furniture. He was looking into what appeared to be a storage room.

Taking a deep breath, he pushed the door all the way open.

The first thing he noticed was the boy's wide-eyed stare. The second was the old man who knelt beside him. Then he saw Dominick Fontanelli.

In a pool of blood.

26

As the old man turned, Bolan realized he was looking at three generations. Guido Fontanelli opened his mouth to say something, but Bolan raised his M-16. The old man nodded. Bolan stepped through the door and into the room. With the M-16 pointed in front of him, he turned and dropped into a crouch.

No one else was in the room. The bleak surroundings spoke of neglect. Dust was everywhere. Guido had smears of dirt on his clothes, and his grandson's face was streaked with dust and tears.

"Who are you?" the elder Fontanelli asked. His voice shook and he struggled to rise. Bolan stepped toward him and noticed a dark bruise on the old man's forehead.

The warrior held a finger to his lips, and the old man nodded his understanding. Dominick Junior started to speak, and his grandfather clasped a gentle hand over the open mouth.

"*Silenzio,*" he whispered, stroking the boy's hair with a trembling hand.

Bolan knelt beside Fontanelli and felt a pulse at the base of his neck. It was strong and steady. He rolled Fontanelli on his side and opened the bleeding man's coat. A bullet hole in the shirt oozed blood, but Bolan was relieved to see it was very close to the edge of the shirt, just above the hip.

He pulled the shirt up and noticed the long gash in the flesh over the hipbone. An ugly cut on Fontanelli's temple also oozed blood, although it didn't look serious. Bolan guessed that Fontanelli was unconscious from a blow, rather than the gunshot wound. He leaned toward the old man and whispered, "Tell me what happened."

While the old man talked about his efforts to help his son, Bolan tore a strip from Fontanelli's shirt, then knotted a second one to it. Wadding a third piece of shirt into a thick strip, he wrapped the wound tightly, knotting the makeshift bandage securely over the gash. When he finished, he realized the old man had asked him a question and stared expectantly, waiting for an answer.

"Sorry," he said, "I didn't hear you."

"Will he be all right?"

"If we get out of here."

"What are you going to do?"

"What I ought to do is shoot you," Bolan snapped.

The elder Fontanelli recoiled as if Bolan had slapped him. "You think I don't know this is my fault? You think I wanted to hurt my son? My grandson? What kind of a man do you think I am?"

"You don't want to know the answer to that."

Bolan turned away. He clapped one hand over Dominick's mouth and patted both of his cheeks. His head lolled from side to side. Bolan felt movement under his palm, and realized Fontanelli was coming around. His eyelids flickered, and he looked up. Glassy-eyed, he tried to speak, but Bolan silenced him with a raised hand.

He removed his hand and bent close. "Can you walk?" he whispered.

Fontanelli nodded.

Bolan climbed to his feet, reached down to help the other man up, then crept to the door. He listened for a moment, then rejoined Fontanelli. He indicated the door down into the shaft. "It's the only way."

Guido looked confused. "I don't know what you mean."

"We have to take the boy and get out of here. Down the stairs."

"But we can't get away..."

"Why not?"

"They found the Blazer," Fontanelli whispered.

"What about the Bronco?"

Fontanelli shook his head. "They disabled it."

"That tears it." Bolan looked at Guido. "You take the boy down to the mouth of the mine. Whatever happens, don't come back here. Understand?"

"But—"

"Papa, listen to me. They'll kill us all. They'll kill Junior. Do you understand?"

Guido sighed and nodded. He took his grandson by the hand and helped him onto the ladder. Bolan passed him the flashlight as Dominick bent and kissed his son. Then he wrapped the old man in his arms. "It's all right, Papa. Just take care of him."

Guido's eyes filled with tears. He looked at Bolan, his leathery cheeks glistening. "I never meant...I am a foolish old man."

Bolan turned away. Watching the old man, it was hard to understand how he had done what he had done, and what had been done in his name. Bolan wondered how someone so frail could have set in motion so much brutality.

He didn't turn back until Fontanelli closed the door.

"What are we up against?" Bolan asked.

"Roughly ten men. Greenway, a couple of deputies, counting Brady, three of my father's old friends and some guys I don't know. I got two of them before they caught me. The New York contingent arrived after we did. I got caught in the open. By rights I should be dead already, but they want to clear everything with their boss, Alessandro Carbone. Thank God for the chain of command."

Bolan frowned. "You'd better. We're going to need His help."

"We got no choice, Belasko. The only way out of here's through them. We'd freeze to death if we tried to run. Assuming they didn't catch us."

"You ready?"

Fontanelli nodded. Bolan handed him the M-16 and several clips, and unleathered the Desert Eagle. He clicked the safety off and tucked the pistol into his pocket. When the Weatherby was empty, he was going to need it fast.

"I'll go first," Fontanelli whispered. He hefted the M-16 and pointed to the door. "My rifle's in the far corner, on the left, just inside the front door. It's the only automatic I saw. These cowboys are a little weak on high tech."

Bolan closed his eyes for a second to clear his mind. When he opened them, he was ready. Fontanelli balanced on his foot, wincing a bit as pain shot through his wounded side. When he kicked out with his boot, the door flew back like a sheet of cardboard and slapped against the wall of the outer room. Fontanelli charged through. Bolan, the Weatherby at his hip, was right behind him.

The M-16 spewed a steady stream of 5.56 mm rounds. Two deputies, frozen in place, looked like bookends, one on either side of the front door. Fontanelli sliced through them with a tight figure eight.

Bolan split to the right. Greenway stood gaping, his right hand caught in the middle of a gesture he didn't get to complete. Bolan squeezed off a shot that hit the rogue sheriff in the right side of the chest. The man spun like a drunken dancer, the hole in his back gushing a fine red rain. He coiled to the floor, and it looked almost as if he were being screwed into the timber.

A hardguy upended a large table to Bolan's right. Cards and cups scattered in the air in a long arc. In stop time, Bolan thought he could see every single card as it tumbled end over end. Two men hit the floor behind the table. Bolan brought the Weatherby around and drilled two holes into the dusty wood. Someone groaned, and he heard the spastic clatter of heavy boots on the floor.

A hand appeared around the left end of the table. A big Colt revolver cut loose with wild .45-caliber slugs. Bolan moved the Weatherby left and fired again. He dived to the floor and crabbed his way to the opposite end of the barricade. He yanked the Desert Eagle free and rolled once more, but the two men behind the table lay still.

Looking back across the room, he saw Fontanelli stumble just as a big, ruddy-faced man with a handlebar mustache aimed a .45 automatic at his back. He fired as Fontanelli fell, and the bullet ripped a fistful of down from the man's coat. Fontanelli rolled over and lay on his back. He swung his rifle back over his head and fired a short burst upside down.

His instinct was sound, but his aim was off. The big man fell back into the bathroom, just under the spray of slugs. A metal mirror on the wall sprouted a half dozen pockmarks. The bare light bulb overhead dripped into the puckered holes as if it were being sucked through to the other side.

Bolan fired the Desert Eagle twice. The first shot ripped a hunk of the doorframe loose, and splinters sprayed over the gunner's leg. The Executioner dropped his aim and squeezed again. He saw the impact of the .44 slug on the guy's inner thigh. The leg jerked, and a thick geyser spouted through the ragged hole in the man's faded blue jeans. He groaned and clapped a slablike hand over the wound.

Bolan rolled again. The change in the angle was all he needed. He found himself staring into the beetlike face and fired once more. The slug slammed into the bridge of the man's nose and cored through his brain.

The sound of gunfire died away. Bolan watched Fontanelli get up off the floor, then snatch his AR-15 from the corner. He tossed the M-16 back to Bolan, following it with the remaining clips.

"Where the hell are the rest of them?" Bolan asked.

Fontanelli moved toward the front door, but Bolan stopped him. "Don't open that."

The slap of wood on wood caused Bolan to whirl. The sound had come from the back room. Before he could move, Junior sprawled through the rear open door. Guido Fontanelli, his hands clasped behind his head, stepped into the front room, followed by a man twice his size. The guy looked to be two or three inches over six feet, and he weighed an easy two-forty.

"Get rid of the guns," the behemoth ordered. He held an automatic pistol to the back of Guido's head. Fontanelli looked at Bolan, then back at his father. He dropped the AR-15. Bolan hesitated, just long enough to draw the big man's eyes, then let the M-16 fall. He dropped the Desert Eagle next to it. The Beretta stayed. If they wanted it, they could come and get it.

When the guns were down, the big man shoved Guido through the doorway. The old man tripped over his grandson and landed heavily on his left side, next to Walt Greenway's body. Guido groaned and tried to raise himself in an uncoordinated push-up, but the effort was too much for his frail arms. He fell back to the floor and lay there panting, his face turned toward the body.

"Hello, Leo," Fontanelli said.

Two more men followed the huge man into the front room. All three were dressed in topcoats, and the striped pants of thousand-dollar suits, wrinkled and muddy from the cuffs up, showed beneath their coat hems.

Leo Fratello shook his feet one at a time. "Fucked up a good pair of shoes, Dom. Pisses me off."

"I bleed for you, Leo."

"You will," one of Leo's companions said. Bolan knew the two men behind Leo. There were differences, three or four inches in height, and maybe thirty pounds, but the faces were close, like before and after in a reducing ad. The DiFalco brothers.

"Shut up, Pete," Leo snarled.

"So," Fontanelli said. It sounded more like resignation than a question, but Leo answered it anyway.

"So, I guess we got to talk about some things."

"What for?" Fontanelli asked. "What's the point?"

"Damage control, Dom, damage control."

"That's Leo's bag, Domenico," Pete DiFalco sneered. "You know that. Mine's just plain damage." He had accented Fontanelli's given name, and the man bristled at the implicit insult to his father.

"No, Pete, your bag is just plain garbage."

The enforcer moved so fast that Leo couldn't stop him. Fontanelli couldn't avoid him. DiFalco slammed a fist into Fontanelli's jaw, knocking him to his knees. "Watch your mouth, shithead."

Fontanelli spit out a tooth. "Come on, Pete, you'll fuck up perfectly good dental work."

"That ain't all I'll fuck up. When I get finished with you, you won't need teeth, real or otherwise."

"You always were impetuous, Pete."

"Shut up, both of you," Leo snapped. "Dom, I got to ask you some questions. I'd appreciate it if you'd answer them straight. No bullshit. This isn't easy for me. You've got to know that. Guido was always good to me, and I always liked you."

"Yeah, Leo, sure," Fontanelli replied. "I love you, too."

"Hey, what can I say?"

"Cut the bullshit, Leo," Pete snarled. "Ask your fuckin' questions. I want to get the hell out of here."

Out of the corner of his eye, Bolan noticed Guido's hand creeping across the timbers like a parchment crab. The sticklike fingers closed around the butt of Greenway's revolver, then lay still. Bolan shifted his weight, getting a little more of his body between the mobsters and the old man.

"Billy," Fratello said, "Take the kid in the back room. And don't hurt him."

DiFalco grumbled something unintelligible and stepped around Bolan to reach for the boy. Guido raised the pistol and fired once. The slug took the top of Billy DiFalco's head off and he fell like a dead ox, landing on Guido's legs.

The ceiling turned red, and clumps of gray matter clung to the old wood for a second before falling to the floor.

"Jesus H. Christ," Fratello muttered.

Pete DiFalco roared and knocked Fratello aside, raising his Uzi at the same time. Bolan hurled himself headfirst, catching DiFalco in the midsection. He knocked the Uzi aside as DiFalco squeezed the trigger. Nine-millimeter slugs chewed into the wall and floor until the clip emptied. The machine pistol clattered to the floor as Bolan snapped DiFalco's arm.

Fratello backed toward the doorway, but Bolan was too fast for him. He snared Fontanelli's AR-15 and ripped out a burst even before he had control. The slugs chewed a ragged line from corner to corner, stopping Leo Fratello dead in his tracks. The mobster dropped to the floor in an untidy heap.

Bolan turned to find Dominick Fontanelli sitting beside his father, cradling the old man's head in his lap, absently stroking his gray hair. Then Bolan saw the line of ugly red holes across the middle of the old man's back.

The warrior stepped out into the cold air. A small hand crept into his, and he looked down at little Dominick. The voice of the boy's father drifted through the door as Bolan moved away, pulling the youngster with him.

Bolan stood quietly with the boy, allowing Dominick a few moments to grieve in peace. They could enjoy a brief respite from the battle, but the warrior knew that Carbone would pursue Dominick with dogged determination. Ruthless people were always willing to spill the last drop of blood. No matter the cost. But until Fontanelli accessed the information that revealed the extent of Mob infiltration into Fontanelli Industries, Bolan would be there at his side. Somebody had to stand hard to keep the jackals at bay.

TAKE 'EM NOW

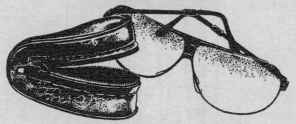

FOLDING SUNGLASSES
FROM GOLD EAGLE

Mean up your act with these tough, street-smart shades. Practical, too, because they fold 3 times into a handy, zip-up polyurethane pouch that fits neatly into your pocket. Rugged metal frame. Scratch-resistant acrylic lenses. Best of all, they can be yours for only $6.99.

MAIL YOUR ORDER TODAY.

Send your name, address, and zip code, along with a check or money order for just $6.99 + .75¢ for postage and handling (for a total of $7.74) payable to Gold Eagle Reader Service. (New York and Iowa residents please add applicable sales tax.)

Remove from pouch

unfold once

unfold twice

and they're ready to wear

GES-1A

GOLD EAGLE

Gold Eagle Reader Service
901 Fuhrmann Blvd.
P.O. Box 1396
Buffalo, N.Y. 14240-1396

Offer not available in Canada.

The past blew out in 2001.
Welcome to the future.

JAMES AXLER
DEATHLANDS®
Northstar Rising

A generation after a global nuclear war, Minnesota is a
steamy tropical paradise of lush plants and horrifically mu-
tated insects. In this jungle, Ryan Cawdor and his band of
post-holocaust warriors uncover yet another freakish leg-
acy of a world gone hideously wrong: Vikings.
